The MONKEY who fell FROM THE FUTURE

Ross Welford

HarperCollins *Children's Books*

First published in the United Kingdom by
HarperCollins *Children's Books* in 2023
HarperCollins *Children's Books* is a division of HarperCollins*Publishers* Ltd
1 London Bridge Street
London SE1 9GF

www.harpercollins.co.uk

HarperCollins*Publishers*
Macken House, 39/40 Mayor Street Upper
Dublin 1, D01 C9W8, Ireland

1

Typeset in Adobe Garamond by Palimpsest Book Production Ltd,
Falkirk, Stirlingshire

Printed and bound in the UK using 100% renewable
electricity at CPI Group (UK) Ltd

PROLOGUE

This story starts around four hundred years from now. Nature has retaken the earth.

Our planet's population, which peaked in 2044 at nine and a half billion, now numbers mere millions.

No one died, other than normally. But almost no one was born, either.

From the moment the lump of space rock burst through the earth's atmosphere and smashed into the ground, and the alien germ that it carried spread round the world on the wind, the only babies born were to the tiny number of people who were immune to the infection.

By the time the germ was identified, it was too late.

Towns and cities that once hummed with the din of humanity now lie silent and empty, winds howling through roofless, windowless buildings covered in ivy. Trees, shrubs and wild animals fill the once-busy streets. Rivers, controlled by humans for centuries, have burst their banks; magnificent bridges that linked cities and even countries are crumbling away; tunnels have flooded; dams have burst; vast ships have broken loose from their

1

moorings and sunk; aeroplanes lie rusting where they last landed; and everywhere millions of cars, vans and trucks slowly decay on roadsides or in damp and dripping underground car parks where bats and wolves and wild dogs live. Medicines are scarce, and lives are short.

Hospitals, schools, libraries; shopping malls, offices, airports and railway stations – all have been smothered by the unstoppable regrowth of nature.

The electronic communications on which humans relied no longer work; computer memories deteriorated long ago; electricity is rare. There's no more petroleum, although some centuries-old engines remain, powered by steam, or fish oil.

And yet . . .

For those who remain, food is plentiful. Housing – once repaired – is free. Homes are filled with the furniture and belongings left by those who lived in what is called the Wonder Age. On the island they still call Britain, it's warmish and wettish; there are many small farms. The survivors often have big families. Small communities are usually peaceful and harmonious. A few cities and ports still stand – Newcastle, Liverpool, Edinburgh, Dover. (London, however – once the capital – is a hellish flooded wasteland.)

And still every child born is celebrated and loved as has been the way throughout humanity's long history.

One such child is Ocean Mooney. She is eleven and lives with her grandmother. This story begins with her.

PART ONE

OCEAN MOONEY'S STORY
NEWCASTLE, ENGLAND
AD 2425

CHAPTER 1

In the summer, the quayside fish mart in Newcastle ends when the old cathedral clock strikes midday. If there's any fish left, I give it to one of the children from the orphanage over the river. Nanny Moo does not mind; if it was not for her, she says, I would be an orphan too.

I noticed the new boy straight away, skipping across the rope bridge high above me. He hardly held the rope sides, looking right ahead and trotting confidently over the wobbly planks. Just watching him made me gulp with fear, but he swung the bag by his side without caring that a single misstep would send him plunging to his death in the river far below.

Since a huge, rusting chunk of the last remaining bridge collapsed into the Tyne a few weeks ago, this is the only way left to cross the water.

A few mins later, I was rinsing my plastic fish crates, and the boy on the bridge was now just metres away from me, whistling as he nailed a poster to a wooden noticeboard. I saw that he was too dandified to be an orphanage boy. His boots were newish, and he wore a long grey coat that was overbig for him, and a round-topped black hat of the sort that was popular during the early Wonder Age.

He saw me staring at him, and I quickly looked away.

'It's all right to look, young paloni,' he said. 'Do y'not want to vada me sticker-bill?'

His words, his accent: he is not from around here. 'Young paloni' I think means 'young woman'. I did want to see his poster, though.

'You should be more guardy,' I said. 'The Brownies do not like people putting up . . . sticker-bills.'

He scoffed and banged another nail in. 'Brownies? Oh, rats to them: I ain't scared o' no muddlin' Brownie. Here – hold these, will ye? Don't wanna put them down in the puddle.'

He handed me a large bundle of rolled-up posters, and took another ready for affixing to the wall behind him.

As if on cue, there was a clottling of horses' hooves from along the quay as a large brown-clad marshal on a tired-looking pony emerged from a side street and hollered, 'Oi! You two! Stop right there!'

The boy did not wait even half a second, but barged past me in his haste to get away, then he turned and grabbed my arm. 'Come on! He means you as well.'

I dropped the bundle of posters and ran after him.

*

6

What would have happened if I had not done that? If I had simply said my apologies to the Brownie and that I did not know the boy in the hat, and I was just here to sell my fish? I suppose I will never know.

You see, until I met that boy, my life was good. Uncomplicated. My grandmother – Nanny Moo – is a fish-filleter by the harbour in Tynemouth. I go to Papa Springham's morning school in Culvercot thrice a week, and I sell fish below the broken bridge on the Newcastle quayside on the other days.

Of course, I could not know, when I ran after that boy, that it would lead to me finding the Time Tablet, and meeting Kylie and Thomas, the children from 400 years ago.

Everyone calls that time 'the Wonder Age', and I went there. I really did.

Let me tell you how.

CHAPTER 2

The boy turned left and ran up the narrow stone stairway that leads from the quayside. We were halfway when the Brownie appeared at the bottom. His pony reared up, refusing to mount the steep, crooked steps. The boy, seeing this, let out a whoop, then bent down to show his bottom to the Brownie before taking the rest of the steps two at a time.

The marshal did not come after us. Instead, he yelled, 'You'd better watch out, you cheeky wee varmint!'

At the top of the steps, the boy turned and fell to the ground, laughing and holding his sides. I was still peeping scaredly round the wall.

'Don't vex y'self,' he said after he got his breath back. 'What they gonna do if they catch ye?'

'Beat me? And you?'

He waved his hand don't-carily as if a beating from a Brownie was no big deal.

I said, 'It may be nowt to you, but I sell fish down there! He may recognise me. You . . . you are reckless.'

'Nope, I ain't reckless.' He leapt to his feet in a single

fluid motion, then went *rat-tat-tat-tat* with his clompy boots on the ground. He swept his coat to one side as he bowed low, tipping the hat forward from his head. It rolled over on his forearm. He caught it in his hand and replaced it on his haystack of spiky blond hair.

'I'm Deucalion Smiff . . . Better known among me more *hintimate* acquaintances as Duke! Pleased to meet ye.'

One of his eyes was dull and motionless, with an old swelled-up scar beneath it; the other was such a bright blue that it seemed to sparkle to make up for its companion's lifelessness. He held out his bony hand for me to shake, and when I took it he pulled me to my feet.

'What's yer name?'

'Ocean. Ocean Mooney.'

He looked me up and down, as though working out whether to trust me. I do not know if he liked what he saw: a smallish girl with freckles and pigtails in an oversized, patched smock and red welly boots. I suppose he did because after a moment he said, 'Come on then, Ocean Mooney – the Brownie's gone now. We've gotta get them sticker-bills back that *you* dropped. They cost me uncle a portion!'

I stood before the poster that this strange lad had nailed up.

MONSIEUR MUSTAPHA B. LUMIÈRE
&
THE CARAVAN OF ASTONISHMENTS
Presents
A RARE TRIP BACK IN TIME!
A LECTURE AND DEMONSTRATION
Including a full-length film IN COLOUR
STAR WARS
Experience the WONDER AGE in style and comfort
TYNEMOUTH FISH FAIR
Salutation Hall, Front St,
11 a.m., 3 p.m. and 6 p.m.
Admission two crowns
CASH ONLY - NO BARTER

'Ever seen a fillum before?' said Duke. 'Y'know – a proper *moovie*?'

I shook my head. I knew what they were, of course. In the Wonder Age, they were everywhere – on people's televisions, on their cellphones and tablets and computers. Fantastic stories with music and 'special effects', which made things that were not real look as real as if you were standing next to them.

'That's a true story, that is,' said Duke, pointing at the title *Star Wars*.

'What? Was it not just made up?' I said.

'Course not. In the Wonder Age, they had spaceships,

and they went to th'moon all the time, and they were always having wars, so it's obvs true!'

I wondered if he was teasing me. Just then, there was a patter of footsteps coming down the stone stairs, and a smallish man in a spensive-looking velvet coat appeared beside us. He was holding the hand of a monkey who was sucking its thumb like a well-behaved toddler, and I let out a gasp of surprise.

'Aha!' said the man, and he clapped his gloved fingers together. 'My fabu-labulous poster. Well done, Duke!' he said. He looked at me and removed his tall hat in the same showy way that Duke had. '*Bonjour, mademoiselle!*'

'*Bonjour, monsieur!*' I replied, and the man's face lit up, although I was finding it difficult to take my eyes off the monkey, who was wearing a tiny sleeveless jacket in the same purple velvet as the man's coat.

'*Mais, mam'selle!* You speak French?' He then gabbled rapidly and incomprehensibly for about half a min, pointing at the poster and gesticulating 'stravagantly. I did not understand a word so I studied the man instead. Neatly trimmed beard, black hair oiled into a tall pompadour, normous eyebrows styled into points, and old, often-mended clothes of rare style and quality. At the end of his speech, he bowed to me again.

Well, this was 'barrassing. Ventually, I said, 'Erm . . . I am sorry, ah . . . *je regrette* . . . ah, my *français* is not very, erm, *bon*.' (My teacher, Papa Springham, would be disappointed, I think.)

'You understand nothing of what I just say?' Monsieur Lumière looked forlorn, and he pouted as though he had just given the speech of his life and no one had heard it.

'Well, I understood *bonjour*!'

He ran a finger beneath his neat moustache. Then his face suddenly brightened, and he was once again the chipper figure from a moment ago.

'No matter. It is a good thing I speak English good, *n'est ce pas*? Allow me to present myself. I am Mustapha B. Lumière. *The* Mustapha B. Lumière! You have met my nephew, Duke. And this,' he said, gesturing towards the monkey, 'is my compani-anion Pierre.' The monkey bowed just as his master had done a moment ago, making me giggle.

Monsieur Lumière jerked a thumb at the poster. 'You 'ave 'eard of me?' he said, his dense eyebrows waggling hard.

'I have now!' I replied, diplomatically.

'Ah, *merveilleux*! And you are coming to my show, I expect. I 'ave never met anyone who is not incredified, transformixed and – ' ow you say? – smacked in the gob by the unbelieve-alieve-abubble show I present!'

'I would love to come,' I said, 'but it is a little spensive.'

Monsieur Lumière held his hands up to his face in stonishment, his mouth forming a perfect O.

'*Oh là là!* But today is your day of lucky, my friend. For I need an *assistante.* Can you ride a bible-cycle?'

'A what? Oh . . . a *bicycle?*' I repeated in surprise.

'*Oui!* The bible-cycle! Another beautiful French invention, like the cinema! I use a form of this vehicle to create the light for my movie show – and you, mam'selle, could be the extra person I need. Help me, and you will see the fillum for free!'

'Yes, please!' I said.

Monsieur Lumière's eyebrows danced. 'All you 'ave to do is pedal. Like a crazy person! You will be perfect!'

He removed his right glove and held out his hand.

'Ocean Mooney,' I said, shaking his hand and marvelling at its softness. Duke slapped his dirty mitt on top of ours. Then the monkey squeaked, jumped up on to Monsieur Lumière's shoulders and added his little monkey paw.

'And now, mam'selle, you can 'elp me further. We are looking for accommo-dommodation?'

Well. That is something I deff could help with.

CHAPTER 3

Once more at the top of the steps, and a short walk between the windowless buildings of the empty city, and we were in front of the old cathedral where the clock was chiming the hour.

A crowd of people had gathered round a long painted caravan. They were stroking its sides and clambering on its thick tyres.

'Make way! Make way!' cried Monsieur Lumière, clapping his hands as we approached. 'All the wonders within this *véhicule* you may see with your own eyes, lays and gennlemen, at the Tynemouth Fish Fair. Come and see the most miracu-laculous marvels of the Wonder Age!'

The colourful caravan was attached to a tractor that looked as though it had been pieced together from at least four other vehicles. It had big wheels, a long bench seat and a closed cabin behind it. Monsieur Lumière hopped up on to the driving seat and opened his arms.

'There is something to amaze everybody. Electrical equipment! Home devices such as the robot that will make tea! *Mais oui, madame!* A fully working gramophone playing music from the Wonder Age. The last remaining desktop computer *in the entire world*! And, of course, a full performance of the greatest movie ever made: *Star Wars*!'

From his coat pocket, he took a handful of paper slips that he gave to Pierre the monkey who was waiting 'spectantly on the front of the tractor.

Monsieur Lumière gestured with his hat to the lettering on the side of the decorated van which said:

MUSTAPHA B. LUMIÈRE'S
CARAVAN OF ASTONISHMENTS

'Oh yes – two for the price of one with a ticket from Pierre!'

People grabbed the vouchers as Pierre moved among them. Monsieur Lumière leapt from his seat and came over to us. 'You see? It will be a 'uge success. And now: all aboard the Wonderbuggy!'

He bent to crank a handle at the front of the tractor, and the engine coughed into life, belching thick fish-oil smoke from the exhaust chimney.

We chugged away from the cathedral, away from the inhabited part of the city, passing the buildings that had crumbled with age, and on to the road that leads to the coast. The three of us sat on the bench seat, with Pierre riding on top of the caravan behind, 'tracting amazed stares from the drivers of the horse-drawn carts and the walkers on the road.

And that is how I rode back home to Tynemouth. Not – as I usually do – hitching a ride downriver with one of the fishing vessels, or taking the new oil-train, but sitting high on a tractor between a strange Frenchman and his nephew with a wide-eyed monkey chattering with 'citement behind me and bouncing every time we hit one of the many potholes in the ancient road.

On either side of the muddy highway, the trees stretched out as far as I could see, with occasional roofs poking above the green canopy, and small farms dotting the mass of green. The afternoon sun was high and glinted off the glass remains of a tower block that once housed thousands of people. Most of the buildings – the houses, the shops, the schools – had long ago been swallowed up by a tide of green, as nature had reclaimed what had once been taken from her. (We call this 'the Bush', and nobody goes there, apart from the salvagers who try to find the stuff that was left by the people of the Wonder Age.)

Duke nudged me and pointed to a huge old boar crossing the road in front of us. It stopped and shook its head angrily at us as we approached, forcing us to slow down, and it bared its broken yellow tusks as we passed, making me shiver. Above us circled a pair of toucans and, as we neared the coast, scores of squealing seagulls appeared.

Soon the road forked at the old petrol station that had given up the last of its precious fluid centuries ago. The left-hand fork goes to the little bay at Culvercot; we took the right one towards Tynemouth and, it will turn out, a whole new future.

Nanny Moo sniffed disapprovingly at the three new arrivals standing nervously on the black and white tiles between the items of furniture packed into our entrance hall. She circled them, hands deep into her apron pocket, while the grandfather clock tick-tocked loudly.

'French?' she said after getting a whiff of Monsieur Lumière's rather pungent cologne.

'*Oui, madame!* Mustapha B. Lumière, direct descendendant of the great Auguste and—'

'Travellin' showman?' she said, without any attempt to hide her disdain.

'Aha! I prefer the term "International Exhibitionist".'

Nanny Moo peered at him over her spectacles. 'You can call yourself what you like, *mon-sewer*. Only I run a respectable establishment here, and—'

'I can pay you in advance, *madame*. A whole month. And I can repair things, such as . . .'

Nanny Moo's attitude changed 'mediately. 'A month? The Fish Fair only lasts three days. I thought you'd be off after that.'

Monsieur Lumière blinked rapidly. 'Ahh . . . we 'ave

some . . . other business in the area, madame. It may or may not be conclu-duded in the speci-fecified time.'

'Other business? What would that be then?' Nanny Moo does like to know what her guests are up to, but Monsieur Lumière was already counting out coins. 'Well, you're in luck. I had a cancellation. There's no discount, mind. Ten crowns a night, breakfast and fish dinner. Hot water is extra, but don't bother askin' cos we're low on oil. I only cook plain. None of your fancy continental stuff. And the ape stays outside.'

I could swear Pierre understood this, for his little shoulders slumped, and he cast his gaze to the chequered floor.

'But, *madame*, Pierre is 'ouse-trained. He uses the lava-tavatory like a man.'

'Oh aye? I expect he leaves the seat up like a man an' all. Well, if he disgraces himself just once, he's out. Is that understood?'

'That, *madame,* will be excel-excellent, *formidable.* I will go and bring the caravan into the yard. Pierre, Duke – come with me.' He bowed, then minced off, his leather shoes click-clacking on the tiles, and leaving me curious about their 'other business'.

There is no business in Tynemouth other than fish.

CHAPTER 4

I was in the yard behind our house, admiring the fancy paintwork of the caravan. There were swirls and loops and little animals and flowers in every colour 'maginable. It was old, and slightly faded – which somehow made it even lovelier. Duke was stretched out zizzing on the tractor's bench seat, his bowler hat over his face.

'You like?' said Monsieur Lumière behind me. 'It is the work of the finest artist off ze kind in Europe. You wish to see inside? Duke – open her up!'

Duke awoke instantly, and jumped down. He flicked a couple of bolts, and the whole back of the caravan sprang open, accompanied by a loud musical chord. Packed into the space were devices of every kind – machines of plastic and metal, most of which I had no idea about their doings.

'Behold!' Monsieur Lumière sclaimed. 'A myriad of marvels! A considera-bubble collection of electrical antiqui-tiquities. And all powered by bible-cycle!'

'Holy ravioli!' I said, pointing at a large black screen. 'Is that a television?'

'*Mais oui!* Unfortun-ortunately, it does not work, but you can imagine, yes? And 'ere we 'ave a "desktop computer", dated to around 2015.'

'And does that work?' I asked.

'Hmmm . . . not exactly. Although I am able to connect it to this device *'ere*, which will allow it to show a moving picture, a video-replica if you like, of word processing in real time so you will see exactly what it was like.'

One by one, he showed me other exhibits: relics of the Wonder Age of the twentieth and twenty-first centuries. A microwave oven, which – he said – worked until quite recently; a 'Teasmade', which is a clock that boils water and makes a cuppa tea; a huge glass-fronted cabinet called a 'vending machine' that serves food when you put a coin in the slot. That, he said, needed repairing. There was a big jug on a plastic base that he called a 'blender', and a 'vacuum cleaner' with a springy plastic hose.

'By the twenty-first century,' he splained, 'most devices relied on silicon chips to work. Saddle-addly, they have all deteri-eriorated and cannot now be replaced. But this . . . this works perfectly!'

He skipped up into the caravan and picked up a box with a large flared horn attached to it, which he carried to an upturned barrel.

'This, my little friend, is the *gramophone* – like all great things, invented by the French. Regard – the large brass 'orn attached to a movable arm on top of this box with a clockwork mechanism inside. Do you see? Duke will demon-emonstrate!'

He lifted up the lid to reveal a simple system of cogs. Duke wound it up with a little handle, and a flat disc started to revolve. Inside a drawer beneath the box were six black 'records': round and flat with a hole in the middle. He put one on the revolving disc, moved the arm with the horn so it was resting on the record and . . .

You will not believe this . . .

Music came out of the horn!

How? I do not know. It just worked, and it was invented back in eighteen hundred and something, and if I did not know better I would say it was magic because that is exactly what it felt like when Duke made music come from the horn.

Monsieur Lumière's eyes closed as he listened to the sound, and his fingers twitched in time. Beside him, Pierre jigged around and clapped his little monkey paws. Nanny Moo came out into the yard to see where the music was coming from, only to be 'mediately grabbed by Monsieur Lumière and spun round in time to the music, as though he had quite forgot that she is his landlady, and he has only just met her.

'Oh, get off me, you fool,' she snapped, slapping his hands away. But she was smiling, so I do not think she minded much.

'Et voilà! This 'ere,' he said, 'is the 'eart of the thing.

My life's work. Salvaged from a flooded museum of cinematography by my great-grandpapa and restored to full working order by 'im and my father. The projector! And 'ere is the fillum.'

He placed a large circular tin can on his lap and eased the lid off carefully. I reached forward, and he patted my wrist gently.

'Hey, hey, no touching! Not without zese.'

From a pocket, he took a pair of cotton gloves and put them on. Only then did he ease from the tin the end of a tightly wound coil of paper-thin plastic. He unwound the strip and held it up, and I saw that it was semi-transparent: a series of windows with colours 'luminated by the light behind.

'This is vair rare,' whispered Monsieur Lumière. 'Vair few fillums in this condition 'ave survived the devastation of time. Most of them 'ave been destroyed beyond use. But a few – just a few – 'ave lasted. I, Mustapha B. Lumière –' he looked up, a dreamy look in his dark eyes – 'bring these fillums to life once more. Tomorrow Duke is out front with the megaphone, and you, my little *assistante*, will 'elp me inside!'

Duke put a different disc on to the gramophone and Monsieur Lumière cocked his head as the music came out of the horn. '*Écoutez!* This is "Rock Around the Clock" by Bill 'Aley and the Comets from nineteen 'undred and fifty-four. This wonderful music was being played more than four hundred years ago! The men and women who were playing the guitars and the flutes and . . . and the timpa-nimpani – they died centuries ago, but we can wind up a machine and listen to them! It is like travelling back in time, no? Travelling back in time!'

All that I have described was earlier today. That evening, Duke and I nailed up the remaining posters round town and helped to carry Monsieur Lumière's exhibits into the hall that he has rented for the three days of the Fish Fair.

I have only known Duke for a few hours, but I like him already. He's skinnier than me, but much stronger, and he dragged the massive vending machine all by himself.

When it is done, we sit on the rear step of the caravan in the yard, and we drink Nanny Moo's fish broth that she sent with us in a flask.

'What is your "other business" here?' I ask. 'After all, this is a tiny fair to visit. You may not make much coin.'

Duke blows on the steaming broth and gives me a sideways glance with his good eye. 'Ye's a snoopy paloni, ain'tcha?'

'I am not snooping,' I say. 'I am just . . .'

I shrug. I *was* snooping, I suppose. Anyway, he gulps his broth and says no more – which of course makes me even more curious.

CHAPTER 5

The first day of the Fish Fair is cloudy and mizzly, and the people who have come to Front Street cast glum looks at the sky. Duke, however, stands on the Wonderbuggy with a grin to rival the sun, in his long coat and bowler hat. His boots have been shined to a mirror polish. Beside him, Pierre is in a matching outfit – even the tiny hat.

The Wonderbuggy and the caravan are parked in front of the Salutation Hall, a wide old brick building wedged between a tavern doing busy trade and an open-fronted shop selling equipment for boats. The hall itself is ancient and well preserved thanks to restoration by the townspeople long before I was born. Its polished double wooden doors open on to a small lobby and then, inside, a large room with uneven oak floors and a raised stage at one end. In stone, above the doors, are carved numbers and words in a language I do not understand.

SALUTATIO AD DEUM
1892

Duke raises a battered tin megaphone to his lips and begins his 'nouncements.

'Roll up, lays and gennlemen! Witness the unparalleled astonishments of the Wonder Age *before your very eyes*! The marvellous *moovie* will start at the same time as the rain – in fifteen minutes!'

He has learned to talk this way from Monsieur Lumière, and he is very good at it. He even imitates his uncle's odd way with long words, saying, 'What you see will be truly unbuffaluffable!'

Next to him, Pierre rattles a tin cup with coins in it, encouraging people to pay the entrance fee. Inside, Monsieur Lumière is showing people round the exhibits.

Nanny Moo has positioned herself near the door with a large vat of oil in which she is frying eel and serving it up on five-cent sticks.

Further up Front Street are stalls selling live geese; there is a troupe of acrobats in colourful outfits who say they are from China (although I have my doubts for they do not look Chinese, and sound as though they come from Middlesbrough). There are singers with guitars, a metal cauldron over a fire making fresh popcorn, and a coconut shy with real coconuts. The air is ripe with the smell of every type of fish product you can imagine: fish oils, fish medicines, dried sprats, pickled herring, live lobsters, cured dogfish skins from Cornwall, crabs from up the coast in Craster, winkles, mussels, jars of jellied cods' eyes, fishing lines, fishing nets, fish hooks of every size, and necklaces of sharks' teeth.

Then there is a crack of thunder, and the downpour starts. Soon people are pushing to get inside out of the rain, and Duke winks at me as if to say, *Told you!*

'Standing room only remaining!' he barks into the megaphone. 'Two crowns per person – give it to the monkey. Please form a *bona* line – the show will start more rapid-iddly that way, *ay fang yew!*'

I move inside the darkened hall, holding a lamp, and there are another dozen or so similar lamps on the walls, emitting the unmistakable aroma of the fish oil that burns inside them. I am supposed to be checking people's tickets, though I have no idea what to do if someone does not have one.

I hear a voice saying, 'Ey-up, Ocean! Got yourself a job, I see.' I hold up the lamp for a better view. It is Sunbeam Dinesh, an older girl from Culvercot, with her father, both smiling and munching on Nanny Moo's fishsticks.

Soon the hall fills up. Monsieur Lumière mounts the little stairs to the raised stage and claps his hands together a few times before the crowd is quiet.

'Thank you, *mesdames et messieurs*, boys and girls! Thank you for coming to see my show. Thank you to my two young *assistants*, and thank you to the good govern-overnors of wonderful Tyne-mooth for allowing me to rent this 'istoric building!'

'Get on with it, you French windbag!' shouts Sunbeam's dad, and people chuckle. Monsieur Lumière is unoffended and smiles as he addresses the voice.

'Ah, monsieur! I, too, would be impatient to witness the wonders that are about to unfold in this empori-oriumum of reverie! My friends, stand by to laugh, to cry, to be transported to a galaxy far, far away as we experi-erience the struggle between two worlds and the journey of the twentieth-century's greatest cinematical hero as 'e overcomes an *evil tyrant*!'

Monsieur Lumière's eyes bulge, and the crowd goes, 'Oooh!'

Someone calls, 'Is it a true story?' and someone else says, 'Course it is!'

'Some of you may know that fillums like these were accompanied by dia-lialogue spoken by the actors, and music and fantastic sound effects.'

Monsieur Lumière now hangs his head in exaggerated sorrow. 'Sadly, the technology to reproduce the sound on fillums is lost to us.' He pauses, then draws himself up again. 'But be not dis'eartened, *mes amis*, for I 'ave located a copy of the *entire* script in a library in Leeds, and I will be deliver-rivering the words myself! I will be recreating the music on this, my antique accordion, and the sound effects will be supplied by your own wonderful imagi-naginations!'

There are unhappy mumblings going through the

crowd. I am not sure they were 'specting a silent film in return for two crowns. Somehow, though, Monsieur Lumière's enthusiasm is carrying him through.

'And now I must instruct my young *assistante*. Ocean – commence with the pedal-eddling! And Duke – switch on the projector!'

Duke and I are in a little booth at the back of the hall. I climb up on a small triangular seat with pedals beneath it. As I push the pedals, they turn a chain, which is connected to a large dynamo that generates electricity. A few seconds later, a white rectangle appears behind Monsieur Lumière, his shadow cast large on it. He heaves a huge piano accordion on to his chest and plays a high chord.

'Lays and gennlemen – I present the greatest fillum of the twentieth century. *Star Wars!*'

I can see the screen through a gap in the wall of the booth and watch, mesmerised, as the story of the spaceships and Luke Skywalker and the evil Darth Vader unfolds before my eyes. Monsieur Lumière shouts the story, tries the different voices for Luke and the princess and growling the voice of Darth Vader – and all accompanied by accordion music that does not really fit but nobody seems to mind. The audience is laughing and cheering.

Duke turns to me with a face-splitting grin and says something that I do not hear over the clatter of the projector.

No one hears when the roof starts to crack.

I spot dust coming from the ceiling, the tiny flecks catching the light from the projector. First a few, then more and more. Then there is a loud splintering noise, a huge dust-cloud descends, and a groan of fear goes up from the crowd.

Some people start to push their way out. Then ceiling tiles come down, followed by a massive chunk of plaster, and a gush of rainwater, landing on people as they shuffle and push and scream.

Two of the oil lamps fall off the walls, spilling their fuel on the ground, and flames flick round people's feet, upping the panic. Someone yells, 'Make way for the children! Get the bairns out!'

On the stage, Monsieur Lumière is shouting, 'Please! Do not panic! Make an orderly exit!'

It is too late. He rips off his velvet jacket and starts frantically beating at the tongues of flame licking the stage.

As up on the screen Han Solo and Chewbacca fly the *Millennium Falcon* through space, here on earth the panicking crowd squeeze through the exit doors.

I stop pedalling, and seconds later the light on the projector dies, plunging the hall into near-dark and causing more panic. I can make out Duke, now trapped in the squash of people, his face flushed and breathless, his hat smoking where a flaming ember has caught it.

Then there is another massive crunch, a noise like *whooomf* and an even louder scream as a huge portion of the roof falls in, bringing the screen down and causing another surge of people trying to get out. I join them as they pour through the door and into the street, coughing and caked in dust.

Outside, I find Duke among the brabble of people. I can hardly bear to look at his head, which is burnt and bleeding. 'Where's me uncle?' he is screaming. 'Has anyone vada'd Lumière?'

'He's still in there, son – it's too late to save him,' says a man.

A change comes over Duke's face as quick as turning up the flame on an oil lamp. Without a further word, he hunches his shoulders and pushes past the people who are still coming out.

'No, kidda! Keep outta there!' shouts Sunbeam's dad, dashing after him, but he is stopped by a smouldering roof beam that falls in his path. It knocks over Nanny Moo's cauldron: the boiling oil sloshes into the entrance and catches fire itself.

'Duke!' I shout. 'It is too dangerous!' It is impossible to make myself heard above the commotion. Nanny Moo grips my arm, and I realise that I was about to run in after him. I turn and, terrified, I bury my face in her greasy apron. I just cannot bear to look.

I am not sure how long I stay like that, but I do notice

when there is a sudden, brief lull in the crowd's noise. I hear someone shout, 'Look!' then someone else cries, 'Help him!' and when I turn I see Duke, both fists gripping the back of Monsieur Lumière's collar, dragging his uncle's limp body through the flaming building into the street.

'Is he alive?' says a voice.

'Keep away – stand back – give him some air!'

'Uncle! Uncle!' yells Duke at his side. 'Oh, please!'

I hardly recognise the body lying outstretched on the ground. His left arm is at a rum angle, his clothes are charred and torn and, strangest of all, his head, which before had been topped with piled-high black hair, is completely bald, with a large cut oozing blood.

'H-his hair!' I say, horrified. 'It has been burned off!'

Suddenly the blackened face twitches, his eyes blink, and Monsieur Lumière starts to cough and retch and then moan in pain. A cheer erupts from the crowd. He raises a hand to his scalp and murmurs, 'My wig!' He touches the cut and winces.

'I fink yer wig may have saved yer life,' says Duke, laughing with relief.

Monsieur Lumière coughs again and then says something like, '*Weppy air . . . weppy air . . .*'

Duke shouts, '*Où est Pierre?* Has anyone seen Pierre? The monkey?'

Oh no . . .

The question is repeated through the crowd of sad, shaking heads.

Everyone had escaped the fire apart from poor Pierre.

*

The fire rages for another hour before the rain and people with hoses and pumps and buckets of water bring it under control.

Dr Mason from Culvercot turns up with his bag of potions. First, he wrenches Monsieur Lumière's shoulder back into its socket with a horrible pop, then he stitches his scalp.

While this is happening, Duke sits dazily on the step of the caravan, a faraway look on his face, turning a tiny bowler hat over and over in his sooty hands.

CHAPTER 6

Two days later, and poor Monsieur Lumière still coughs a lot from the smoke; his arm is still swelled and burnt. He stays abed, nursed by Nanny Moo and Doc Mason, who visits daily on his black horse.

The *Chronicle Newsletter*, which Frau Schwartz pins up on the board in the little library in Culvercot, reports the story as:

Monkey Dies in French Film Fish Fair Fire

Monsieur Lumière's life's work – his Travelling Cinerama, plus all the wonderful (and, all right, not-so-wonderful) exhibits – was nearly all destroyed by both the fire and by the water used to put it out.

Duke has hardly said a word since it happened. His own burns were quite light, although his big spiky hair now has patches where it burned away. The grinning, tap-dancing joker that I had met under the bridge only a few days ago has become a grey-faced and silent ghost.

*

The fair has wound down for the final night. Some people are singing in the distance and others are getting into boats to head upriver. Here and there, oil lamps prick the gathering darkness across the water in South Shields. Nanny Moo went to bed ages ago; Monsieur Lumière is fast asleep, thanks to what Doc Mason calls 'a herbal tincture' made from jimsonweed, which he grows himself.

The gaudy Caravan of Astonishments escaped the fire. Duke and I hitched it up to the Wonderbuggy, and he drove it back to our yard. I can hear him now in the near-empty caravan fiddling with something. It is a cool night, and I warm up a cup of fish broth on the stove to take to him.

He is bent over on the floor of the caravan, with bits and pieces of some gadget or other spread out round him. He looks up when I approach and manages a weak smile – the first time I have seen him smile in days.

Duke points with a screwdriver to the bits on the floor. 'Electric toaster,' he says. 'If I can fix it. One of the heating elements is done for, but y'know . . . it might work.'

I sit down next to him. 'I liked the gramophone best: the music. It is a shame about the computer. And the film.'

Duke grunts. 'Aye, well, that's the worriment, ain't it? People wanna be 'stonished. It was the Wonder Age, after all: it has to be wonderful. But, since the last silicon chip died, well . . .' He pauses. 'Everyfin has to be mechanical. That's what me uncle says anyhows.'

I am not sure what he means by this. Duke sees me looking puzzled.

'It's like this,' he says, twirling the screwdriver expertly in his fingers. 'Our last hope of reinventing computers vanished when the North University flooded a few years back. They'd worked out how to clone the very last remaining computer chips, but . . .' He shrugs. 'Never happened, did it? Every last one was ruined.'

We sit in silence for a few moments, watching the lights go out on the other side of the river. I am certain there's something Duke is not telling me, but I cannot work out what it is.

'Is he really your uncle?' I say. 'Only you do not . . . you know . . .'

'Look alike? I know. He's me ma's half-bruvver. Me real pa was from Cornwall – but I never met him, although Uncle says he was a good, honest man. That's why I have his last name – Smiff. Ma died when I was little, and me stepfather took me to sea wi'him. He was . . . not a good man.' He points to his dead eye, and I gasp.

'He did that?'

'And worse.' Duke swallows hard. 'Mega worse. Uncle met him in Calais a few years ago and saw what was going on, so he . . . he won me back.'

My mind is racing at what Duke could mean by that. 'How? How do you win someone?'

'Uncle offered him money at first. All the coin he had to get me away from him. But Pinker – that's me stepdad – quite liked having me around to bully and abuse. It wasn't much money anyhows: the travelling show has never been what you'd call successful. So Uncle challenged him to a game o' cards: winner gets . . . me!'

By now, it is dark outside. Duke pauses to sip his fish broth. In the light of the oil lamp, I can see his eyes glistening with tears. I say, 'That was lucky then – that he won the card game.'

Duke wipes his eyes and half smiles. 'I'm not sure it was luck. Uncle's a showman, see? You ever seen his card tricks? I reckon a tiny bit of, um . . . *legerdemain* may have been involved.'

'What's leger . . . what's that then?'

'It's sorta cheating, but sorta not. Anyways, he won me. I've travelled wi' him and Pierre ever since. I owe him me life, Ocean. And now I wanna repay him.'

We sit in silence a bit longer, then he drains the mug with a slurp. 'Bona soup,' he says. Then: 'Wanna see summink?'

He springs to his feet and opens a little chest at the back of the caravan. From it, he brings out a white plastic tube. 'Vada this,' he says.

CHAPTER 7

The plastic tube is about as long as my forearm, with stoppers at each end. There are labels that have been torn, little square stickers showing that king from years ago, scribbles and smudges all over them. Duke pops off one of the ends and tips up the tube.

Inside, rolled up and wrapped in tissue, is a very old newspaper. As Duke spreads it out carefully on the floor, some of the pages crack a little, and they are quite discoloured, but it is still perfect readable. Thanks to the floods and fires and neglect that came with the Great Silence, newspapers are very rare – and yet here is one on the floor in front of us.

'Whatcha fink?' says Duke. 'Have y'seen one o' these afore? Do y'know what it is?'

I nod. 'Papa Springham brought one to school. They were popular in the Wonder Age: they told everyone what was going on in the country and the world. Then they sort of died out. Where did you get this?'

Duke chews his bottom lip as if he is weighing up whether to tell me. 'It was Pinker's,' he says. 'Me stepfather. I, ah . . . borrowed it off him when I skedaddled wiv Uncle.'

'You stole it, you mean?'

'I was tryna read it one day – y'know, tryna teach meself how. He din't like that.'

'He . . . he did not like you learning to read? Why not?'

'Dunno. Said I would learn too much and be more savvy than him. He was a very clever man. He had . . . big ideas. Computers and stuff.' Duke paused. 'So anyways he beat me. That's when I got me bad ogle.' He points to his eye. 'It was the last time. So, when I left wiv Uncle, it was one o' the fings I nabbed. Put it in the bottom o' me bag and, well . . . here it is. I don't s'pose he's even noticed it's missing.'

The date on the front is 20 July 2023. On the front page is the name of the newspaper, *Chronicle*, in faded blue letters and below it, in black, it says:

TOON SIGNS YANK STRIKER FOR £40M

There were some rum words back then. There is a picture of a young man in a striped shirt. I read the words below.

'It's about football,' says Duke. 'That fing there means forty million pounds. That was a lotta money. Uncle says that people who were good at football were very rich.'

'Why?' I say, and he shrugs.

I turn the pages, wondering why a seaman like Duke's stepfather would have something like this.

More strange stories. Someone's 'electric kettle' exploded in Wallsend; there were tales of policers arresting people for being drunk and causing fights; 'nouncements of brand-new cars for sale; and a picture of a new restaurant in Newcastle with food from Brazil. I could read about the Wonder Age forever and not get bored, but Duke is waiting. When I turn the next page, he taps his finger on a picture with a story below it.

It shows two children, about me and Duke's age, and one of them – a girl with huge hair and big white teeth – is holding up a rectangular screen with wires coming out of it. Also on the table in front of them is what looks like a young tree in a pot.

I read the story.

TV Fame for Culvercot Cousins!

Two north-east cousins will get a taste of fame at the weekend with a trip to Tyne View Studios and an encounter with Geordie television legends Andy and Des.

Thomas Reeve, 11, and his Australian cousin, Kylie Woollagong, 13, of Tiverton Close, Culvercot, will appear on the famous duo's hit BBC show *Ministry of Mystery* where Kylie – a teenage computer whiz – will show off her incredible 'Time Tablet'.

The device, a much-modified tablet computer, will, Kylie claims, be able to send and receive pictures and sound from 400 years in the future!

After the show, she says, she will bury it in her garden "two metres east of a yew" – specially selected as a long-lived tree. She hopes it will be discovered before July 2425 when, she claims, a solar megastorm will create a unique radio-magnetic field sufficient to warp space-time.

Sounds incredible? Kylie doesn't think so.

'It is amazing!' says the Australia-born genius, soon to be a pupil at the new North East Foundation Academy in Hexham. 'As long as someone finds it, we'll be able to see directly into the future and maybe even talk to people then. If it works, it'll happen on live TV. I just hope our house is still here!'

A professor of astrophysics at Newcastle University, Astrid Larsson described the youngster's theory as 'interesting', but declined to comment further.

Andy & Des's *Ministry of Mystery*, BBC 1, Saturday 7.30 p.m.

When I finish reading, I see that Duke is smiling. 'That, Ocean, is why Uncle and I are here,' he says. I give him a puzzled look.

'Look, no disrespect, but the Tynemouth Fish Fair ain't exactly the biggest carnival around, is it? And it's pretty outta the way.' He points at the newspaper story again. 'We came here for this. Culvercot is just up the road.'

'Your "other business"?' I say, and he nods.

'Just 'magine if we could find this Time Tablet! It would be a sensation!' Duke looks up, his eyes wide with 'citement. 'Fink of it, Ocean! Fink of all the fings they could do in the Wonder Age. The motorcars, the aerialplanes, the wars wi' spaceships . . .'

'I keep telling you: I think *Star Wars* is made up.'

'Who cares? They carried all o' the world's knowledge on a little device in their pocket. If they could do that, Ocean, what's to stop them creating summink that really *could* link wi' their future?'

'And does your uncle know about this?'

'Of course. He just doesn't believe it can work. He told me today he wants to stop travelling, stop the show. He's lost his sense o' wonder, Ocean.'

'And you think this will bring it back?'

The light in Duke's good eye tells me I am right.

'The Time Tablet, Ocean, is buried beneaf a yew tree near here. All we have to do is discover where Tiverton Close was.'

PART TWO

THOMAS REEVE'S STORY
TYNESIDE, ENGLAND
AD 2023

CHAPTER 8

My cousin Kylie and I travelled into the future live on Andy and Des's television show. Everyone saw the whole thing.

All right, not the *whole* thing. Not the bit when we were actually *in* the future. I think if people had seen that bit then it wouldn't be so controversial: people would have had no choice – they'd simply had to have believed it. As it is, a lot of people still say it was a stunt. They saw the monkey appear; they saw me and Kylie disappear. It's all on YouTube. And still some say it was a hoax – just a big elaborate prank.

It's made Kylie and me famous, which neither of us likes, but Mam says that so long as we keep our heads down and stay off social media then that'll all go away.

It's going to be hard, I realise that. Kylie's new school (the North East Foundation Academy, out near Hexham) will probably help her: you know, hanging out with other megabrains and doing loads of brainy stuff. We'll see.

So, before you ask: Kylie and I will not be doing interviews. We will not be on social media talking about our adventures with Duke Smiff and Pierre the monkey, and Duke's evil stepdad, or answering any questions about how we pulled off 'the illusion of the century', or taking part in the Netflix documentary that's being made and for which we've been offered a 'life-changing' sum of money. To be honest, I think I'm done with having my life changed.

But, before we stay quiet forever, this is what happened. What *really* happened.

It's the story of how we prevented the end of humanity as we know it. Or probably will anyway: Kylie's working on it. I know – you and I are doing projects on the Romans, or learning long division, while Kylie's designing 'laser bees' to destroy a meteorite.

You're going to love her. Certainly more than I did at first.

CHAPTER 9

A FEW WEEKS EARLIER

Cousin Kylie leans back, making Mam's old office chair creak, and puts her Doc Marten boots up on the desk like she owns the flippin' place.

'Check this out, Tommo. I'm calling it the Time Tablet, and it's gonna make us famous?'

Us. That's the thing about Kylie: she thinks I like her when I really don't. And I *really* dislike being called Tommo. And the way she's just taken over our family. *And* the way that everything she says sounds like a question? A bit like that? Mam said she's just lonely because of her super-intelligence, and that the 'everything-sounds-like-a-question-thing' is just her way of 'seeking validation of her feelings', and I just nodded because it's the easiest approach when Mam talks like that.

So, when Kylie mentions her time-whatnot, I arrange my face into an expression that I hope shows mild interest. You know, interested enough not to be hostile, but not so interested that she's going to take up a lot of my time talking to me about it all. Trouble is, it never seems to make any difference: she'll talk and talk in her annoying Australian whine regardless of what my facial expression is.

Mam and Dad say she's a 'genius', but that I shouldn't mention it because it makes her self-conscious. Personally, I reckon that if you're a genius you should be able to tell if you're getting on someone's wick, but what do I know? I'm just your average Year Sevener.

The thing Kylie's pointing at (at least, I *think* she's pointing at it: there's so much junk – cables, wires, keyboards, dirty cups, sweet wrappers – on the desk that it's hard to tell) is a tablet computer like an iPad only a cheaper version. It's got bits attached to it with Blu Tack and black tape, and I must have accidentally dropped my 'interested' face because she says, 'Ah, don't look like that, Tommo, mate? It's not quite finished yet? Listen, let me explain . . .'

Oh, here we go.

Four weeks ago, Cousin Kylie – full name Kylene Toora Woollagong – had burst through our front door in Tiverton Close, tripped over, banged her head, sworn loudly and then given me a bone-crushing hug, even though I'd never met her before. She hugs as though she's learned how by reading about it.

She immediately set about changing my life. In fact,

she probably changed all our lives, but we'll get to that soon enough.

Dad, who had picked her up from the airport, stood on the front path between two enormous suitcases, saying for the tenth time that inviting Kylie to stay with us and leave her home in Australia was a Brilliant Idea and So Much Fun. Behind him was the old sports car he's been restoring that I was supposed to get first ride in, but that he'd just used to collect her.

Mam came through from the kitchen, wiping her hands on a tea towel and smoothing her hair down. She had make-up on, which was odd for a Saturday morning, her hair was tied up, and she had on the nice top from last Christmas. When she caught me looking, she'd said, 'What's wrong, Thomas? You don't get a second chance to make first impressions. I want my niece to feel welcome. Can I suggest you reintroduce your hair to the idea of a brush?'

Kylie has released me from her hug, and I'm looking at her in something like awe, and feeling something like fury.

Here's the thing: our house is pretty small, and our family works fine with the three of us: Mam, Dad and me. Four if you include Korky the cat.

'There's just not room!' I said to them both when they'd announced Kylie's visit. ('Visit'? Are you kidding me? A visit is when you go to stay with someone for a few days. Kylie is actually coming to *live* here.)

'Don't be daft, Thomas,' said Mam. 'We'll clear out the spare room. I don't need a home office any more. It'll be nice to have a girl around the house. Give me a break from you fellas, eh?'

And so it was that all the junk from the spare room (among other things: an exercise bike, a broken armchair, an ancient printer, boxes of CDs and DVDs, a filing cabinet and a gross fur coat smelling of mothballs that Mam won't throw out because it belonged to Gran) ended up . . . guess where? Yup: in *my* room.

Kylie is enormous. Much taller than me, with a wide back, big hands and a large crown of unruly rust-coloured hair, puffed up by the ride in the open-topped car. Her spectacles are the size of glass saucers resting on her broad nose, and her big white teeth look like she's borrowed them from a pony.

'Kylie!' coos Mam. 'Look at you – haven't you grown! Come on in. How was your flight? Are you hungry? I've made some soup. Do you want to call your mum, let her know you've arrived safely? Thomas – take Kylie's coat, will you?'

We sit at the kitchen table, Kylie eats three bowls of soup and Mam keeps saying, 'You must be so tired after the long flight.'

I can't stop myself. 'Why? What's tiring about sitting down and watching movies for hours while someone brings you food?'

I get The Look from Dad, and refocus my attention on my soup.

Mam keeps peppering her with questions. It's as though she's scared that if she allows a moment's silence to occur, then Kylie will get up and say, 'Sorry, I've got to go back to Australia?'

All the while, I'm sitting opposite this girl-mountain and feeling like our little house had shrunk the moment she barrelled through the door. Then I notice that Korky – normally very suspicious of new arrivals – is wrapping herself round Kylie's ankles like she's her NBF.

Okay, quick family tree. Kylie's mum is Mam's sister, Ailsa, who moved to Australia before I was born to be with Kylie's dad. I've never met them apart from occasional awkward FaceTimes at Christmas and stuff. And now Kylie is to live with us before she starts at a boarding school in Northumberland for 'students of exceptional potential' – in other words, geniuses. Her mum's coming back to England later in the summer. (Mam said Kylie's dad 'went walkabout' with a roll of her eyes, so I guess that's a touchy subject.)

'More soup, Kylie? Well then, Thomas will show you your new room, won't you, Thomas?'

Dad has been joking about Kylie smuggling house bricks in her luggage. 'You'll need a hand to carry the suitcases upstairs,' he says.

He needn't have worried. Kylie hauls the biggest one

up to the spare room where Mam has made up the bed with my favourite *Star Wars* duvet cover.

Kylie points at it. 'Who is that anyway?'

She doesn't recognise Darth Vader!

This is going to be a long visit.

CHAPTER 10

'Who's *that?* It's . . . it's . . .' I'm almost speechless. 'It's Darth Vader!' I say, pointing at the main figure. 'And that's Obi-Wan Kenobi, and . . . Don't you know them? "Use the force, Luke . . . let go!"' I say in my best Obi-Wan voice.

Kylie hauls the heaviest suitcase on to the bed, which creaks in protest. 'Course I've heard of them. Some kids' film, iznit?'

I am blinking in astonishment, but I'm distracted when she pops open the suitcase to reveal not clothes and shoes, as I'm expecting, but two big bubble-wrapped computer screens, assorted keyboards, cables, a large console of plugs and wires, computer mice (at least one decorated like a real mouse), boxes of disks, and other tools like screwdrivers and tweezers, and a soldering iron.

She sees my puzzled expression. 'This is what I do, Tommo? I mean, instead of watching dumb films about Obi Wonky Bobby or whatever his name is?'

Mam's words from a couple of days ago come back to

me. 'You'll find her unusual, Thomas. Her brain operates on a different level. Be kind.'

So I say, 'We've got Disney Plus! You can watch them whenever . . .'

Kylie waves her hand as though my words were annoying flies. 'Thanks but no thanks,' she says. 'I don't really do stuff like that. Not with this project to complete. Time is not on our side, Tommo – depending on your understanding of the nature of time, hey? Now, do you have any extension cables? And maybe a multi-socket plug?' She tuts. 'You really do not have enough electricity outlets here, do you?'

I feel myself bristling. Just who the heck is she to come in here, criticising my favourite film and our house in her stupid accent?

'We have plenty of sockets, actually. You just have too many—'

I'm interrupted by Mam appearing in the doorway. She's holding a looped electrical extension cable and a box of plug adapters.

'You two getting on all right? I've brought these up for you, Kylie. We really don't have enough plugs up here for you. Your mam said you might need some extras for your, erm . . . computery things.'

'Thanks, Aunty Mel. I was just saying the same thing to Tommo, wasn't I?'

Mam laughs. 'Tommo! Oh, isn't that funny, Thomas?'

I'm saying nowt. I think that counts as *being kind*.

Mam continues. 'So, when you're unpacked, I thought we'd drive up to town, you know, show you around a bit, see the local . . .' She tails off because Kylie is shaking her head.

'I don't think so, Aunty Mel. You see, I have to get this all set up tonight, and . . .'

'Surely that can wait, love?'

'Yes,' I chipped in. 'You can do it later.' Mam smiles at me, thinking I'm being super-friendly. To be honest, it's not the prospect of Kylie's company that made me say that. It's because a trip to Newcastle always ends with eating the world's best fish and chips by the river, and not even a strange Australian cousin can change that.

A few hours later, I'm sighing to myself and wondering why I even bothered persuading Kylie to come with us.

She has crammed the top of her hair into a baseball cap; the rest billows out the sides like vast furry earmuffs. Her dad is Australian Aboriginal so her skin is browner than mine; still, she somehow seems paler, like a coloured T-shirt that's been through the wash too often. Probably it's all the time she spends indoors on her 'special project'.

And now we're by the River Tyne, and nearby is a group of students. One of them has a guitar and is singing some old song about rocking around a clock, and everyone's clapping along. It has to be the coolest thing ever, but Kylie seems miles away, staring upriver at the Tyne Bridge.

'What do you reckon, Kylie?' says Dad on his way back from the chip shack. He nods towards the bridge. 'Just like Sydney Harbour back home, eh?'

She looks at him like he's mad. 'This isn't a bit like Sydney Harbour. Although the bridge is similar, I suppose . . .'

Dad just laughs it off, but I'm furious. 'It had the same designers and builders, you know? And our bridge came first!' (My geography project on local landmarks was 'highly commended' last term. I may not be 'gifted', but that's not nothing, is it?)

We've got our cardboard boxes of red-hot cod and chips with about a ton of salt and vinegar, and in between fistfuls of chips Kylie talks about possibly the only thing she seems enthusiastic about, so far at any rate.

'. . . and so there's the paradox. Time travel is possible *in theory*. Even Albert Einstein said so. But "in theory" has to be tested, and if the *theory* is correct then some sort of exchange of information across space-time must be possible. So, in conclusion . . .'

My mind wanders – honestly, yours would too – to the students sharing beers and the swooping, squawking kittiwakes, and I see my glorious, happy summer wafting away like the voice of the girl with the guitar.

Dad's doing his best, but his expression is the same as when he turned up with Kylie earlier: a sort of fixed, baffled smile.

Kylie says, 'The only reason nobody's done it yet is that conditions in space have prevented it. But, if my calculations are correct, then there's every chance that the forthcoming solar super-flare will create a burst of radiation . . .'

I glance across at Dad. The lines at the sides of his eyes crinkle a tiny bit, and I know it's not just me. That's quite a relief.

'Well, that's nice for you, Kylie,' says Mam. 'Everyone needs a hobby. Anyone for more ketchup?'

'It's getting pretty late, guys,' say Kylie, yawning.

It isn't. It's six thirty. I haven't even finished my chips, there's the possibility of ice cream as well, *plus*, the pool table inside the café has just become free, and I know that Dad would love a beer and to play deliberately badly so that I can win.

Mam goes, 'Aww, Kylie, love. You must have terrible jetlag. Freddie, go and get the car, eh? We can finish our chips on the way home.'

'I also need to start work on my Time Tablet project.'

'Your what?' says Dad, getting to his feet.

Kylie's eyes widen in surprise. 'My Time Tablet project? I've just been telling you about it, Uncle Freddie? Were you not listening?'

She sounds hurt, and Dad quickly says, 'Oh that! Ha ha, yes. Sorry. Of *course* I was listening! We all were. Fascinating. *Doctor Who* and all that.'

She ignores him, away in a world of her own again. Probably wondering who Doctor Who is.

'The future,' says Kylie. 'Just imagine the advances that will have been made by then. Flying cars, space travel, medical breakthroughs, weather creation. Just think what we could learn, Tommo? And all thanks to my Time Tablet! By the way, Aunty Mel, is there space in your backyard to plant a tree?'

Plant a tree?

What the heck does she want to plant a tree for?

CHAPTER 11

OCEAN

Culvercot is about a kilometre up the coast from Tynemouth, and it is now very small, although back in the Wonder Age it was a busy seaside town. All the buildings that are occupied are gathered round the crescent-shaped bay. These have been maintained and lived in for many years. Go further than about two streets away from the seafront, however, and the decay starts with empty houses, dangerous, crumbling brickwork and the remains of a few, long-abandoned motor cars. This is what we call the Bush, where no one really goes. Everything has been salvaged years ago; there are large holes where the roads have collapsed.

Duke and I have passed the tumbledown church that overlooks the Long Sands with its broken steeple, and crossed over the new oil-train line to find ourselves in the Bush, and already I am a bit nervous. The trees have closed behind us like a heavy door. It is darker and much quieter. We stand in the middle of a road that was once, I guess, a fairly 'portant street.

Most of the old motorcars have been cleared away. According to Papa Springham, as the population dropped during the Great Silence, them who were left tried to keep the main roads clear. Unwanted motorcars were stripped of anything valuable – engine parts, glass, rubber, electronics, even mirrors – and then towed away to dumping grounds. In the end, there were too many cars and not enough people to move them, and the vehicles were simply abandoned on the street and inside garages.

Where we stand, most of the trees remain, although some have died or blown over across the road. New ones are growing between the buildings. Hundreds of years of falling leaves and other waste have created a thick, spongy layer on top of whatever the road was made of. Brambles, nettles and grasses poke through.

Beyond the rows of trees that run down either side of the road, almost invisible beneath ivy and other climbing plants, are houses – hundreds and hundreds of them in every direction. Here and there are huge clouds of tumbling white flowers and smelly yellow cup-lilies attended by clouds of buzzing insects. The windows are nearly all missing – some salvaged many years ago, the rest broken by growing branches or the weather.

Duke flaps away a fly and squints again with his good eye at the piece of paper I am holding: a hand-drawn map that I copied from an old book called *TYNESIDE A-Z 1968* that Frau Schwartz, the librarian, found for me.

'I fink we may have gone past it, Ocean,' Duke says.

I walk ahead, determined to find the 'Tiverton Close' mentioned in the newspaper story that Duke had shown me. We are climbing over a rotting tree trunk when I say, 'Stop!'

Duke freezes, seeing the huge snake only a second after I do. Two metres long and as thick as my leg, it slithers past us and into a doorway with no door.

'Poisonous?' asks Duke. I can detect the wobble in his voice, though he is trying to disguise it. His fingers tighten round the spade we have brought.

I do not know. All I do know is that Britain used to have very few native snakes, but as people became less able to look after their pet animals they released them – including exotic reptiles from other countries. Most died without specialised care; some did not. The weather was a little cooler back then; now that it is warmer, some animals can survive, like the toucans and lizards. And big, fat snakes.

'Look, maybes we should go back?' I say.

'Oh my hat!' he exclaims. 'You frit, ain'tcha? Come on – just a few more mins. Show me the map again.'

Duke is faking his bravery, I can tell, but I do not mind. We have come further into the Bush than I have ever been before, and much further than Nanny Moo would approve of, especially if she knew what Frau Schwartz had told me.

'I hope you're not going into de Boosh,' she had said as she handed me the book of maps, and I lied smoothly that I was not. '*Ach* – good. Only de Bikpik has been seen again, not far from there.'

I felt a shiver go through me as I remembered the hog with broken tusks that had crossed the road the day I met Duke. Bikpik is a wild boar that for all my life has roamed the Bush between here and Hadrian's Wall. Everyone has heard of him. (There are tattle-tales that he eats stray dogs and naughty children, which I do not think I believe.) I tried not to display any emotion to Frau Schwartz.

'There was another child attacked last month,' she said. 'In Morpeth. He lost his whole hand to that beast! Bit it clean off. Poor boy lucky to be living.'

Now Frau Schwartz is well known for exaggerated tales and gossip. Still, I could not hide the wobble in my voice when I telt her, 'Oh dear. Good thing I am going nowhere near the Bush then.'

I have said nothing of this to Duke, who has now stridden ahead. 'This way, I fink.' I run to catch him up when he stops.

'What's that noise?' he says.

To our left is a rustling in the bushes. My heart starts to beat so hard I wonder if it can be heard. There is definitely something – something largish – only a few metres from the road, hidden by the high grass. The vision of the huge boar with its broken tusks flashes into my head again.

'It is all right,' I whisper. 'They are nocturnal.' (I am not even sure this is true.)

'What are?' says Duke.

Whatever it is moves again, slightly nearer, and several more seconds pass with Duke and me silent and still with terror. Then it is coming towards us, running at full speed, and I am about to scream when it breaks cover.

We look into the startled brown eyes of a small deer. It stops for a second and then turns back the way it came. Duke and I both breathe out together.

'I . . . I thought it was a . . . oh, never mind,' I gasp. Then we both laugh: a demented cackle of relief.

Where we stopped is a break in the trees. A row of rusting, skeletal cars beneath ivy and some crooked streetlamps mark out a short street of smaller houses, all with collapsed roofs and brickwork shrouded in green.

'Is this it?' I say. 'Is there any way of being sure? I mean, the streets will still have signs, surely?'

We locate the corner of the street by a low wall with a right angle and start to kick away the ivy and chop at the vines with the spade. Soon a cracked plastic panel is revealed attached to the wall, the faded letters still discernible.

CLOSE

'It must be,' says Duke who is working from the other end. He reveals

TIV.

'It is! All we gotta do now is find the . . .' He stops and points. 'That's it!'

We are looking right at it. The yew tree towers behind a house in the middle of the street, taller than the roof: a vast dark evergreen with a rounded top.

'How do we get into the back?' I say as we walk nearer to the house.

Compared with most of the other houses, this one seems a bit less ruined. Where the house wall ends, there had been a passageway leading round to what was once the back garden. Only every space is completely choked with weeds and thorny bushes.

Duke grins like he has an idea. Putting the spade down and lifting his leg, he smashes his heavy boot against the front door. With a crunch and a cloud of dust, and the buzz of a massive, angry hornet, the rotten wooden door collapses inwards.

He steps back for a mo, then rushes at me, pushing me through the doorway as a large piece of wall falls from above and thumps into the ground 'zactly where I had been standing.

CHAPTER 12

'Thank you,' I say to Duke, and he shrugs. We watch the dust settle and try not to 'magine what might have happened.

Inside, the house seems hardly touched by the passage of time, although it is clear that assorted animals and birds have been calling it home for centuries. Beneath a layer of dust and leaves, there is still the remnants of a carpet, which tears easily under my feet. There are even pictures on the walls, and some on the floor where they have fallen down. Ivy has found its way in through the window frames and twists down the stairs, the staircase and bannister rail.

Here and there are patches of the patterned paper they used to put on their walls. A coat, stiff with age and mildew is draped over the stair post.

Duke and I gaze around, open-mouthed in 'stonishment. 'Look at this,' I say, pointing to a faded, framed photograph. It shows a girl with big teeth and a smaller boy, both smiling at the camera. 'It is them from the newspaper, for sure!'

'No one's been in here,' he breathes. 'Like – no one.'

It is as though the last occupants, at some point during the Great Silence, simply closed the door behind them and left.

I swallow hard. 'Do . . . do you think they died here?'

It is possible. Salvagers tell stories of houses they have entered to find skeletons still wearing the rotting clothes of the Wonder Age. In fact, it is one of the rules of salvaging that if you come across a skeleton it must be removed and buried properly. A rule, though, that is often ignored.

I shudder and notice with relief that the front room, at least, is bare, apart from a low table and a sofa covered in dirt and mould. 'Look,' I say. 'Some stuff has been salvaged. We are unlikely to find skellies.'

Still, it is too creepy to explore further. Instead, we move quickly through the hallway of the house to what was once a kitchen at the back. Here the windows are intact, although covered with mould, and in the green-shrouded light there is more evidence that salvagers have been here at least once. Cupboard doors are open, but some plates and cups remain. A metal sink and draining board are covered in a thick layer of dust with animal tracks and rat droppings on the surface. I pick up a mug from the sink and wipe years of dirt off it.

The words on it are:

Duke nods, satisfied. 'We've found it, Ocean!' he says before turning and kicking the back door down the same way he had the front and then waiting a few seconds in case this, too, would dislodge loose bricks. There, at the end of a waist-high lawn of weeds, is the massive yew tree.

Up close, the tree is ancient and gnarled. Its grey-brown bark has thick ridges, and creepers and vines hang from the branches like furry green necklaces. Looking up, I can barely see the top of the tree, while below my feet the roots spread out, sloping into the ground.

Duke digs into his pocket and studies his compass. *Two metres east of the yew tree.* He takes two long strides, lifts the spade in the air and thrusts it down in the ground.

'Ow!' he cries as the spade bounces back. 'Roots. Everywhere. Whoever this Kylie character was din't account for root-spread when she buried the fing. We need better tools.'

There is a shed to our left, almost completely obscured by ivy, and it takes us a few minutes to uncover the door, which opens with a strong shove. Duke pokes his head in and gives a long whistle. 'Vada the kushti car!'

I peer over his shoulder to see a two-seater motorcar

– the best I have ever seen. You can tell it was once dark green from patches that are not rust-orange.

'Wanna come for a ride?' says Duke. He squeezes in the shed door and climbs into the driver's seat, making *vroom vroom* noises like the cars of old. Meanwhile, I have spotted a rusty axe hanging from a hook in the wall.

Back outside, we slash at the grass and weeds to reveal the earth, and start to hack at the roots with the spade and the axe until we have managed to dig away the first few centimetres.

That much takes half an hour.

It gets a little easier after that, but we still keep hitting roots, and after another hour we are only the depth of a spade blade, and both of us are running with sweat. I am ready to give up, but I dare not say this to Duke who is attacking the ground as though it is his mortal enemy and making twice the progress I am.

'I need to rest,' I say.

There is a stone bench beneath some vines. I sit, hearing the noises of the Bush: the low drone of hornets, the rasping chorus of parakeets, several woodpeckers . . . and only a few metres away the panting, rhythmic mutterings of Duke.

'Take *that* Pinker . . . this is for the time ye punched me . . . go on, take it . . . never again . . .'

He has to keep stopping, but his strength keeps going.

'You swine . . .' he continues. 'You absolute and complete – *hey, Ocean!*'

At the bottom of the hole, now two spades deep, is something whitish, not a stone and not a root.

It takes another half an hour's digging till we can lift out what we have found: a large steel canister, which we ease from the hole together. Exhausted, we prop it up on the pile of dug-up earth. I start to wipe it down with leaves while Duke fans himself with his bowler hat.

It is shaped like a longish drum, about twenty centimetres wide and thirty long. Duke crouches down and rubs the surface with his sleeve. Stamped into the dull steel are words saying TIME TRAPPER and then, below them, as though added on another occasion, it says:

AS FEATURED ON ANDY & DES'S

Ministry of Mystery

BBC 1, 26 JULY 2023

CHAPTER 13

THOMAS

'TOMMO!' Kylie bellows from her room. She's been here a month, and she doesn't even bother to come to the door now. She just uses her lung-busting voice to shout for me. Like a mug, I get up from my bed where I was grabbing a peaceful few minutes, watching a favourite scene from *Star Wars III: Revenge of the Sith* on the iPad, and put my head round her bedroom door. I immediately recoil from a wave of warmth carrying a thick scent of sweat and cheese Doritos. She doesn't even look up.

'Look – the Time Tablet,' she says.

The 'piece of junk' would be more accurate, I say to myself. Out loud, I say, 'Oh really?'

She pushes her specs up her nose and starts. 'Let me explain,' she says.

Five baffling minutes later, I say, 'Will it work, I mean, for real, Kylie? Because if you ask my opinion it all sounds a bit . . . I dunno . . .'

'Ambitious?' says Kylie, typing on the big black keyboard. 'It certainly is, mate. Certainly is.'

'Well, that's not the word I was thinking of . . .'

'Bold? Daring? Visionary?'

'I was thinking more . . . deranged?'

She stops typing and swivels her chair to face me again. 'You think I'm crazy?'

'Well, yeah . . . a bit,' I say with an apologetic shrug. 'It's not necessarily a *bad* thing, Kylie. But you have to admit this, this . . .' I wave my hand at her three screens.

'This world-changing and audacious project?'

'Yeah, that. It's all of those things, definitely. But it's also – and don't take this the wrong way, Kylie – insane. You can't connect with the future because the future hasn't happened yet.'

She tilts her head and smiles a bit condescendingly. 'Only if your concept of the passage of time is linear, Thomas.'

Oh, here she goes.

'Like a line? This happens, then this happens, then this happens?'

'Well, yeah. That's how time passes. Yesterday, today, tomorrow and so on.'

'Not necessarily! It *may* be that time passes in a more . . . circular way. Just ask the Australian Aborigines. They have a thing called "Dreamtime", sometimes expressed as "Everywhen" . . .'

'Everywhen?' I repeat.

71

'Yeah. Like "everywhere", except instead of a place it's time . . .'

And she's off. The next few minutes is 'Everywhen' this and 'space-time' that and ancient civilisations and the boxed-in thinking of modern society. My attention is distracted by Korky who has taken to sleeping in Kylie's room – mainly, I think, because all the computers make it so flippin' warm in there. Right now she is stretched out luxuriously along a shelf above some humming boxes with blinking lights. I mean, I know she's just a cat, and it shouldn't matter, but it annoys me. Anyway, when Kylie pauses to take a breath, I have to pretend that I've followed it all. I say, 'So what you're saying is that this will definitely work?'

She looks at me over the top of her glasses like a disapproving librarian. 'I'll make it real simple for you, Tommo? When you look at a star at night, you're actually time travelling? It's taken so long for the light to reach earth that you're looking at something that happened hundreds – even thousands – of years ago, yeah? Well, my project does exactly the same, only the opposite, and so we'll be looking at the future.' (That's simple, is it?)

Kylie paces up and down her room (which is only four paces anyway). 'So no, Thomas. It won't definitely work. Just possibly. Even if something is highly unlikely, it remains possible, doesn't it? Listen: you know how babies are made, don't you?'

'Well, duh. Of course.'

'Okay – so you know that it is *highly unlikely* that you were even born. The sheer chance that brought the cells together to form *you*, rather than anyone else, was millions, billions to one. But it still happened, didn't it?'

I nod, and that seems to be enough.

She turns her attention to the device – more like a collection of bits – all laid out on the worktop that almost encircles her room.

'First of all, an electronic calendar,' she says, pointing to a tiny round box the size of a 2p piece. 'I've disabled the display. Waste of battery. This thing just keeps time, ticking over year after year after year, powered by this.'

She indicates a larger box, the size of a small book, connected by a wire to the calendar. 'This is a battery. Fully charged, it'll power a laptop for a few days, and it'll power my little calendar for maybe a thousand years. These two in turn are connected to this –' she points to a black rod like a pencil – 'which communicates with Permasat – the solar-powered satellite launched last year that'll last indefinitely. You musta heard of that?'

'Sure,' I lie.

Kylie beams and holds up a cheap-looking tablet computer. 'Well, then! Everything's attached to the tablet here, and all the connections will be vacuum-sealed in polyethylene and put in waterproof non-degradable steel, and we'll hide it somewhere where it can be found if you're searching for it.'

Nodding, I murmur, 'Why?' and her smile vanishes.

'*Why?* she repeats. 'Jiminy, mate! If this works, we'll be talking to the future! We can find out what happens to us – climate change, space travel! Just think: we can find out what we need to know to stop climate change.'

I shrug. 'Don't we kind of know that anyway?'

Kylie is getting agitated, but she isn't put off. 'Use your imagination? It's the future, Thomas – imagine their cities! Imagine the advances they'll have made. Personal drones, robot servants, hologram holidays, trips to the moon . . .'

So far, it sounds like a mash-up of every comic and sci-fi film I've ever seen, but I don't say that. Instead, I say, 'Awesome!'

'And best of all – medical advances. Imagine their hospitals! We'll be heroes, man, Tommo!'

'We?'

'I need you too. I'm way too shy to go on telly on my own.'

'To go on *telly*?' I tell you, this is getting stranger and stranger.

'You haven't seen the posters up in school? Have you heard of Andy and Des?'

Have I heard of them? What a dumb question.

Kylie takes out her phone and shows me a picture.

CHAPTER 14

BBC Television presents
ANDY & DES'S
MINISTRY OF MYSTERY
LIVE from Tyne View Studios,
Newcastle-upon-Tyne
Andy and Des want to meet YOU!
The BBC is searching for the BIGGEST
MYSTERIES in the Northeast!
HAS YOUR DAD SEEN A UFO?
Has your granny met a ghost?
Are you and your twin super-psychic?
Or do you simply have a crazy invention that
you think will make us laugh?
Call us now on 07971 878 472
Or email celia.taylor@bbcproductions.co.uk

'I've already called them,' says Kylie. 'They love the idea of the Time Tablet?'

'They do?'

'Sure they do! Who wouldn't? This Celia woman's the producer. She's coming round to see us.'

'Us?'

'Of course us. Like I said, I'm not going on telly on my own, am I?'

'But . . . but, Kylie. This Time Tablet thing isn't going to work, is it? For real?'

'Well, it might. Just gotta make a few minor adjustments, that's all. By the way, I've found the perfect hiding place as well. It needs to be dry, away from the elements – you know, rain, wind . . .'

'I know what the elements are, Kylie,' I snap. 'Where then?'

'Underneath us. Right there in our back garden! These houses are gonna be here forever, aren't they?'

I shrug. 'Dunno, Kylie. How old are they now? How old are houses anyway?'

'Well, whatever. Trees last for hundreds of years. I mean, even if they knock the houses down and dig the trees up, someone'll find my tablet and keep it, won't they?'

'I guess . . .'

'Oh, come on, mate? Be a bit more positive?'

'Yes, Kylie, for sure!'

'That's the spirit, Tommo!'

Her fingers dance on the keyboard in a blur. (I have to say, annoying though Kylie is, her typing is very, *very* fast. She can type almost as fast as she can talk, and she makes hardly any mistakes.)

'What do you make of that?' she says, pointing to her screen and grinning smugly. There's a picture of a tree. She taps her keyboard again. 'And what's *that*?'

'It's a much smaller tree, Kylie. What's this all about?'

'Arriving here tomorrow, Tommo. A sapling . . .' She pauses and adds, 'That's a baby tree, Thomas.'

'I *know* what a sapling is, Kylie. Do you think I'm stupid?'

(As it happens, I didn't know what a sapling was, but I wasn't going to let her know that, was I?)

'Not just any sapling, though? This, my little pommy friend, is yew.'

'Is me?'

'No! Not you, yew!'

'Who?'

'Not who, yew! Yew. Y-E-W, yew. The tree. *Taxus baccata*. Commonly called the English yew. It's one of the world's longest-living trees. I mean, a yew that's nine hundred years old could still be middle-aged.'

I'm still wondering what this has got to do with Kylie's stupid Time Tablet when she types again and another page comes up on Amazon.

'TIME TRAPPER'

Made from high-grade stainless steel, this time capsule will keep your letters, photographs and other mementos securely sealed for up to 500 years GUARANTEED.

Certified leak-proof and resistant to every natural hazard.

Perfect for family and community time capsules.

As featured on **ITV News**, **Blue Peter**, *Netflix's* **History Lords** *and many other TV programmes.*

The picture shows a shiny metal cylinder full of documents, and there's a little film of a family grinning as they put one in a hole they've just dug.

'I get it,' I say, feeling pleased with myself. 'You're going to bury the Time Tablet.'

I know, I know. It's like she's Long John flippin' Silver or something, and she's got a chest full of treasure.

Kylie slow-handclaps. 'Well done. And the tree,' she adds, 'is a marker. There's room in the back garden. I've already asked Uncle Freddie – he says it's fine?'

'Where in the back garden?' I say, an uncomfortable feeling rising in me.

'Oh, just past the shed at the back? You know, where's there's that open space?'

And now I remember. She'd even mentioned planting a tree the day she arrived, that time we were eating chips on the Quayside. *She's been planning it all along.*

I'm out of my seat and yelling before I even know what I'm doing.

'You can't! You can't! That's where my pond is!'

Kylie looks puzzled. 'There's no pond there, mate?'

'Not yet there isn't. But I was going to do it. And it'll have newts and . . . and frogs, and goldfish and stuff!'

Kylie puffs her cheeks out. 'Phew, I'm sorry, mate? I've ordered it all now. It's arriving tomorrow.'

Mam and Dad are not sympathetic. Thing is, I should probably have told them about my plans for the pond. I'd been thinking about it for ages. But I thought it would be much more effective if I worked out a complete plan before presenting it to them. You know, designing it (square, round, oval . . . I wanted round), building it, digging it (60 cm deep minimum), cleaning it, costing it and all the rest. Then I would look responsible, and Mam and Dad would have to say yes.

Thing is, it's all still in my head. Meanwhile, blimmin' cousin Kylie has just breezed in and said, 'Hey, Uncle Freddie, Aunty Mel, can I dig a hole in your garden and plant an everlasting tree next to it for some stupid megabrain idea I've got?' And they've just gone, 'Ooh, you're so clever, Kylie. Why not?'

I feel tears at the back of my eyes again, and I storm out of Kylie's room because I'm not going to let her see how upset I am.

I hear her calling, 'Tommo! Mate, what's wrong?'

CHAPTER 15

OCEAN

Monsieur Lumière sits at one end of the polished oak table that almost fills our front room. It is his first time out of bed for days. His arm is in a sling, and his head is bandaged. His face seems thinner, his eyes saggier. I realise that his coal-black beard, swept-up eyebrows and moustache were, along with his wig, all part of the show. They are now grey, and his shiny brown face has turned pale and rough with white stubble. His eyes keep flicking to either side as if he has lost something; I think he is missing Pierre.

Duke calls, 'NANNY MOO? Are you . . .'

'Oh aye, I'm coming. Honestly. Forty kilo of mackerel is not going to fillet itself, you know, less so if I have to take time off to listen to you lot mithering on about the Wonder Age or whatever . . .' She comes through, still muttering, wiping fish scales off her hands with a wet cloth, and sits down impatiently on a dining chair. 'Well? What is it?'

Duke holds one finger up in a *wait* gesture while he bends down to the chair next to him and, with his other hand, lifts up the metal canister we dug up which he places on the table in front of him. Duke catches my eye and then with his thumb he flicks open two catches on the lid.

'Behold, *lays an' gennlemen*,' he says, his voice rising as though he is addressing an audience. He reaches into the box and brings out a package wrapped in several layers of plastic.

Beneath the wrapping is an orange-and-yellow layer, which, unfolded, becomes a large carrier bag with the word 'Sainsbury's' on it. (It was a massive shop that sold every food you could imagine from everywhere in the world. Everyone knows that.) From the orange-and-yellow bag, Duke extracts a flattish plastic box. Written on the surface are letters, faded and barely readable.

Duke reads aloud as I look over his shoulder.

IT'S GONNA BE A WILD RIDE
KYLIE WOOLLAGONG
AD JULY 2023

I do a quick calculation in my head – AD 2023. The year now is 2425. This box was sealed up 402 years ago. That is twenty-one years before the meteorite struck that ended the Wonder Age and began the Great Silence.

I think: *The person who did this will have had no idea at all of the tragedy awaiting them.*

The lid of the box is tightly shut with four hinged metal fasteners. Whoever sealed this thing up all those years ago was dedicated to the task. I imagine it was this 'Kylie Woollagong'.

I have the 'stinct feeling that soon, and closely connected with this silvery-metal box, nothing in my life will be the same. Indeed, that nothing in the whole world will be the same. Why do I feel that way? My palms are sweaty, and I wipe them on my smock. Suddenly Monsieur Lumière – who till now has been quiet – eases himself to his feet, puts his good hand flat on the lid and says, 'Wait!'

He allows the pause to grow. 'You have done well to discover-over this, but whatever comes next,' he says, ominously, 'may affect not only your lives, but the lives of billi-illions of people in another age.'

So he feels it too? 'Cept it makes no sense. 'People in another age?' What on earth can he mean?

Duke grins, shy-like. 'I fought you said this would never work, Uncle!' he teased. 'Anyway, we could present it at a show. You know, Monsieur Lumière's Grand Time Tablet or summink? You could make plenty moolah.'

A smile spreads over Monsieur Lumière's tired face. '*Mais non*, Duke. No, no, no. This is for you! You must present the show. You found it, after all.' He sits down again heavily, and waves his hand at us to continue. I ease off the metal clasps. The lid of the plastic box pops loose with a tiny sigh of air.

The first thing we see is a large photograph. The colours are not faded at all, although the picture has become a tiny bit fuzzy.

Duke shifts to get a better look. '*Oh là là!*' he exclaims, only not in a French accent, which makes me smile. 'A real-life photo-fingy.'

It shows a girl with dark eyes, glasses, big white teeth and twisted hair, maybe fourteen years old. Next to her is a younger, smaller boy; both are grinning nervously. They are seated in a brightly lit room in front of two older men who are holding their thumbs up. All are dressed in the style of the Wonder Age. Behind them, on one side, is a large window through which is visible the unmistakable curve of the Tyne Bridge, while above them is a sign bearing the same lettering as was on the mug in the house in Tiverton Close.

Andy & Des's
Ministry of Mystery

I gaze at the photograph for a full minute, and the questions just do not stop flooding my mind. Who are these people? Was the photograph made at the same time

as the box was sealed? And then I see it: barely readable
in the bottom right-hand corner of the picture.

26/07/23

Monsieur Lumière taps the numbers lightly with his
finger. 'So you see? This is the date. Twenty twenty-three.'

I point at the picture. 'This must be Kylie Woollagong,
do you think? She is the only girl. My guess is that these
two are Andy and Des.'

I turn the photograph over and read aloud the tiny
printed words on the back: a message to us from more
than four hundred years ago.

CHAPTER 16

Dear friend,

This picture was taken when my cousin Thomas and I appeared on television in 2023. Soon after it was taken, I created this box — a 'Time Capsule'.

I buried it in our garden. If you are reading this in 2425, then the first part has worked.

I look up and see that Duke's jaw is hanging open. At the end of the table, Nanny Moo's lips are pursed in disbelief.

Everything in this box is an experiment. If my calculations are correct, then in 402 years' time a solar megaflare will release a burst of radiation of sufficient intensity and precision that communication will be possible between me here and you there.

The Time Tablet has been vacuum-sealed

to prevent decay of the silicon chips and CPUs, etc.

Does that make sense?

Duke nods. 'It'll be the world's only silicon chip if it's still working!'

If you're reading this in the future, awesome!!! Your world will be SO MUCH MORE ADVANCED than ours. We could learn such a lot!

Thomas and I will be in the television studio in Newcastle for a live broadcast of Andy & Des's **Ministry of Mystery** at 8.00 p.m. on July 26.

The signal will work on two occasions only.

The first is on July 26. You can be positioned anywhere within about 20 km of the Tyne Bridge in Newcastle, England.

The second occasion is the following day. Then the signal will be much weaker, and you will require a combination of iron and water to make a connection.

See you on telly!

Good luck, future person!

Kylie Woollagong xxx

And Thomas Reeve

The last name was added in different handwriting.

I turn my attention to the plastic box where there is something the size of a large, lumpy book sealed all round with plastic. Duke picks at the plastic with a clarty fingernail till the plastic coating becomes loose, and he removes it to reveal the mirror-like screen of a tablet computer, exactly like the ones they had in the old days. It is stuck to a white plastic rectangle, the two things connected by wires that have been roughly soldered into place. Across the top of the tablet, above the screen, is attached another thick rod like a pencil with tiny glass dots, which may be lights, although they are not glowing.

This, then, is the Time Tablet. It looks very much as if it was assembled by an amateur, and I look again at the picture of Kylie Woollagong.

I turn the device over carefully and use some of the strange, blue gum to attach the photograph and instructions to the back. I would not want to lose them.

There is a button, slightly indented. Presumably it is an 'on' switch. My finger hovers, then Duke reaches out and touches my hand.

'Not yet,' he says.

All three of us stand, transfixed by the strange contents of the box. Nanny Moo's chair scrapes on the floor, and she stands facing us, hands on hips, shaking her head.

'I've known some tall tales in me life, but this? This takes the cake.'

Monsieur Lumière looks baffled and murmurs to me, 'There is cake? Why?'

Nanny Moo goes on. 'It's the most 'diculous thing I ever heard. Here's what happened if you ask me. Many years ago, a child played a prank. That's it! If she could see you now, believing her nonsensical gribbling, she'd laugh her own bottom off. The very idea! If this is how you propose to pay for your lodging and medical care, *mon-sewer*, I fear I and Dr Mason may be in for a long wait. Now, excuse me, I have mackerel to attend to. Duke, Ocean – please come and help.' She taps the side of her head. 'Monsieur Lumière, I think that fire has adversely affected your noggin.'

Her outburst has left us all a little deflated.

'What if . . . what if it ackshly *does* work . . .?' says Duke, perfectly echoing my own thought.

Monsieur Lumière laughs, and his eyebrows leap up his forehead. 'Well, then – we can warn the people in the Wonder Age of the disaster that awaits them if they do not take action against the meteorite bearing the extinction bug! Everybody-ody is a winner!'

Nanny Moo snorts disbelievingly. 'The claim of every cheat and mountebank in history,' she mutters, but Monsieur Lumière seems unoffended.

'Ah, madame, 'ow quickly we forget. The Wonder Age was more than just impossi-bubble inventions. Those aeroplanes were not just for vacations – they carried medicines for exampupple. Ships transported food. The internet – you know about the internet?' We all nod. 'It distributed the greatest thing of all. Do you know what that is, Ocean?'

His voice had grown louder, like it did when he spoke to a crowd, and I became a bit nervous.

'Chocolate?' I quaver. I know it is the wrong answer as soon as it comes out of my mouth, but I have heard about chocolate, and I would love to try it.

'*Non! Non, non, non!*' He throws up his hands. 'Not chocolate. *Knowledge.* And that knowledge 'elped them to build the biggest, most proper-osperous society the world 'as ever known. Where people might live to be an 'undred or more.' He pauses and waggles his eyebrows at me. '*And* eat choco-locolate!'

I stare at him and Duke, unsure I have understood properly. 'You . . . you mean we can stop the Wonder Age from . . . from stopping?'

'Precise-lisely! If it works, it will be an act of supreme mercy, *n'est-ce pas*? If you can communi-unicate with the past, you can tell them 'ow to avoid the tragedy that is 'eading their way, *non*?'

Nanny Moo tuts loudly. 'There'll be a tragedy heading *your* way if I don't get some help with this mackerel,' and she stomps off.

It has not taken long for everyone to seem to know about me and Duke's plan.

Nanny Moo still thinks it is a mad idea. I got a scolding for heading into the Bush, and another reminder that Bikpik the boar had been seen again, but she is probly just trying to scare me. Still, I am saved from thinking about it too much by Duke who I can hear coming since he won an antique skateboard from Sunbeam Dinesh in a swimming race between the remains of the two old piers that used to enclose Culvercot Bay. There are few roads or paths smooth enough to use the skateboard much; nevertheless, Duke has taken to using it where he can, specially on the path leading to our house.

He dumps a pile of papers on the bench next to me.

'Holy gladioli! You did it!' I gasp. He smirks back at me.

'I have to give the skateboard back, but I fink it'll be worf it.'

In exchange for returning the skateboard, Sunbeam's dad, who has an ancient mechanical printing press and a supply of equally ancient paper, agreed to print a poster for our show.

A BOWLED EXPERIMENT IN TYME
Com and vada the Wonder Age FOR REEL!
THE OLD SEAFRUNT CHUCH
CULVERCOT
July 26
SHO STARTS 7.30 P.M.
Admishun one crown
MONNEY BACK GARANTY!

'That is excellent,' I say to Duke, even though his spelling is off. I find my voice wobbling a bit because seeing it 'nounced on paper makes it seem real. Then I say, 'Duke. Do you think this will really work?' and he goes quiet. He takes off his bowler hat and bites the rim while he thinks.

'How would I know?' he says at last. 'But I've already seen more o' the world than most people. So I know that sometimes the fings that seem most unlikely can be true. I met a woman once who could tell if anuvver woman was expecting a babby by smelling her breath, *and* if it was a boy babby or a girl babby. I met a tin miner from Portugal who could do the hardest sums you'd give him in his head, faster than you could work 'em out on paper. So the way I look at it is that "unlikely" and "impossible" are like two cheeks of the same bum, and we're tryna navi-gavigate the crack between them. Does that make sense?'

I laugh, and he says, 'All right then. Let's start putting these sticker-bills up!'

CHAPTER 17

THOMAS

I'm seething. I mean, really. If I was a cartoon, I'd be turning red with steam coming out of my ears.

I hadn't even wanted to go on the stupid TV show in the first place! Every time I thought of being in the TV studio with Andy and Des and everybody watching at home, my stomach would turn over with fear. But, you know, I got over it. Kylie wanted me to, so . . .

Be kind, Mam keeps saying. 'You'll hurt her feelings if you tell the truth, so just pretend.'

So I 'conquered my fears' and 'stepped up to the plate' and said I would do it. And now I'm actually a tiny bit excited.

Then the stupid producer Celia called and told Mam and Kylie that our bit in the show was being moved in the running order, and that there wasn't enough time to have me on as well, and that it would just be Kylie.

Just Kylie. After I've told all my friends. Mam's bought me a new shirt and trainers to wear . . .

I said some horrible things about never wanting to do it in the first place, and how the whole Time Tablet thing was made up anyway. One or two of them may have been directed at Kylie. Of course, Mam and Dad took her side and told me I was being childish. And so . . .

'Have your tea in your room, Thomas,' said Mam, which I wouldn't mind except she's confiscated my laptop and my phone. Opening my bedroom door, I can hear them downstairs. Dad is laughing as Kylie says something about what 'he' said, and I'm guessing they're talking about me.

Don't be paranoid, Thomas. They might not be. I can talk to myself quite firmly sometimes. It doesn't work this time.

And then – don't ask me why, I don't know – I open the door to Kylie's room and – braving the thick air – stick my head in. Something is leading me on and it's not jealousy, or spite, or . . .

All right. It might be a bit of them. I never said I was perfect.

In front of me, Kylie's long trestle table, the one Dad made for her, is slightly bowed under the weight of all the equipment on it. If there's any order to the array of cables and screens and disk drives, then it's lost on me.

The so-called Time Tablet is in the middle, and it's plugged into the big main screen. There's some transfer of data going on – even I can tell that. There are a few progress bars slowly creeping across the screen and a column of data scrolling up at such speed that I can't see anything, but I wouldn't understand it anyhow.

My first thought is just to rip all the cables out and push over the whole stupid set-up. But, angry though I am, I know that would just get me into further trouble. Besides, I'm eleven years old. That really is the sort of thing a five-year-old would do. You know: have a screaming tantrum and throw things.

Instead, I find my hand being drawn to the computer mouse, the one that actually looks like a toy mouse. I waggle it. The cursor on the screen moves to the top left of the scrolling-data column, highlighting an X, and I click. I don't even look, and when a purple dialogue box pops up saying,

**DO YOU WANT TO STOP THIS
DATA TRANSFER?**

I click okay.

I know, I know. I'm being dumb, and mean, and – honestly – I don't want to wreck the whole thing. I just, I dunno, want to create a bit of bother for Kylie because she's caused more than a bit for me. She's turned my life upside down, and now she's downstairs laughing about it.

With my mam and dad. And my cat probably.

I mean, it's only computer stuff. It's not as if any long-term damage can occur, is it? She'll spot the error and put it right, or – most likely – it won't make any difference at all.

And, if I feel at all guilty, then that feeling disappears when I hear the *Star Wars* theme coming from downstairs, and I know they're sitting down to watch a film. Without me.

Seconds later, I'm back in my room when I hear Mam's footsteps on the stairs, and then her head comes round my door and smiles a bit sadly.

'Wanna watch *Star Wars*?' she says.

'Which one?'

'*The Force Awakens*.' She knows it's my favourite.

Seems like I'm forgiven.

I apologise for what I said to Kylie, which is easy. She laughs a lot at the film, and I *think* she even cries a bit at the end, which I don't because I've seen it about ten times, but still . . . I forget about my little act of sabotage. Completely. Well, until the next day.

Next morning, the whole house trembles as Kylie comes thundering down the stairs, shouting, 'Get your new runners on, Tommo! Today's the day you're going on the telly!'

She bursts into the kitchen and narrowly misses

treading on Korky's tail. 'Oops, sorry, bud. I realised how upset you were yesterday, Tommo. So I've just spoken to that silly old producer Celia. I told her if you don't go on then I don't go on! It's too late for them to dump the whole item, so she said yes!'

'You did?'

'Course I did, Tommo. It wouldn't be the same without you, would it?'

I feel really small. I kind of want to tell her about what I did in her room last night, but she's in such a good mood, and what she's done is really kind so . . .

I don't. Besides, what am I going to say? I don't even know what I did or if it's even important. It probably isn't.

It's tonight.

Me and Kylie's big night.

Here's how it's going to work. Later today, a car will arrive at our house to take me and Kylie and Mam and Dad to Tyne View Studios, which is the location for the live TV show. First, we do a 'dry run', which is like a rehearsal, then we have snacks and stuff in something called a 'green room', and then we're live on television. Mam and Dad will be in the audience.

'Here, check this out,' says Kylie. She tosses me her phone, which is showing tonight's TV guide.

CHAPTER 18

Andy & Des's
MINISTRY OF MYSTERY
BBC 1 7.30 p.m.
*Join Andy and Des for more
mind-bending miracles.*
This week:

- The spirits of Borley Rectory: Ghost-hunting in Britain's most haunted house.
- Real or fake? The UFO mystery of Kielder Water.
  PLUS
- A trip to the future: meet Thomas and Kylie, the North East's very own junior time travellers . . . *or so it's claimed*!

CHAPTER 19

The big clock on the wall of the studio says almost seven thirty.

The day has been awesome! Andy and Des have been super-friendly and completely normal. Des said he had a pair of trainers like mine at home. We've chatted to them and done photos with them during the 'dry run', everything.

It's obvious, though, that no one – not even Andy and Des – thinks that the Time Tablet is actually going to work. Instead, they're presenting it as a funny story about a megabrained teenager's ambitious science project, and they're making out like I've been encouraging her.

The studio is decorated with stars and planets, and there's the *actual* TARDIS from *Doctor Who* (which they let us look inside, but it's just an empty box – you probably knew that). Then, when they've interviewed me and Kylie, they're going to play the *Doctor Who* music and *the real Doctor Who* (that is, the actor who plays him) will come out of the TARDIS to talk about time travel! It's all happening in ten minutes, and my mouth is dry.

Kylie and I are standing out of the way of the cameras and cables that snake across the floor, and my heart is beating so hard that I'm sure the noise of it will be picked up by the little microphone that's clipped to my shirt collar. I'm longing to take a selfie, just with Kylie, but we were told to leave our phones in the green room.

Next to me, a young man whose name is Foo (or something like it) has headphones on and is holding a clipboard with the script on it.

Foo turns to us and winks. 'You okay, Thomas? Kylie?' And I nod, trying hard to swallow my nerves. Kylie doesn't respond: she's prodding the Time Tablet she's holding and tutting.

I peep round the side of the thin wall that I'm standing behind. On TV, it looks like it's made of bricks, but it's really just a flat board, painted to look like bricks. The studio set is dominated by a big sofa in bright blue with a massive TV screen behind it. Above it hangs a neon sign saying,

Andy & Des's
Ministry of Mystery

The studio floor seems like it's polished wooden planks, but it's stuck-on vinyl. At least the coloured rugs are real. The windows look out over a high Newcastle skyline, with the lit-up Tyne Bridge and the winking lights of the Quayside. A make-up artist is brushing powder on the boys' faces. (That's what everyone calls Andy and Des, by the way: 'the boys'.)

Then an older woman called Pat, also in headphones, appears and starts shouting. 'We're coming out of the titles VT in thirty seconds. Boys, stay on your marks there. Applause, applause, everyone, please. Camera Two, you should be in position? Thank you! Emma on the follow spot, take them all the way to the two-shot on Camera One and then cut to the wide. All right, everyone?'

Someone else says loudly, 'Stand by to go live! In five, four . . .'

Then the familiar music starts, and a disembodied voice comes through the speakers positioned round the studio.

'*It's time once again to scratch your heads and wonder out loud! Get ready for the most mysterious, the most marvellous, and yes, the most miraculous time of the week! But first meet your hosts, the Men From the Ministry of Mysteryyyyy . . .*

'*AAAAndy and Deeeeeees!*'

The show has started! The boys come down the stairs in between the seated audience who go wild with applause.

Des says, 'Good evenin'! Hello! Hi, everyone!'

Andy says, 'Welcome to the show, and ee, it's a good 'un tonight, eh, Des?'

And so on. Kylie and I aren't the first item, so I feel myself relaxing a bit. I glance at her. She's still stabbing the Time Tablet. Her glasses have slipped down her nose, and her face has scrunched up like it does when she's concentrating. The telly people have put make-up on her, which I've never seen before, and it does make her look prettier, but I don't say that in case she asks what was wrong with her before.

She's furiously tapping the screen of the Time Tablet and muttering, 'Something's gone wrong, Tommo.'

'Oh dear,' I say. 'Is it going to be okay?'

I have a horrible surge of guilt that this may be because of me. *Can she tell from my voice? Do I sound guilty?*

It is my fault, surely? That thing I did out of spite last night. I swallow hard.

We watch the whole show from our position in the wings. There's an interview with a 'professional ghost-hunter' and a fake-looking film of a haunted house that Andy and Des are *so* funny about, even making the ghost-hunter laugh. There's an item about a spaceship that supposedly landed in Kielder Water a few years ago and two men, a father and son both called Geoff, who said they'd captured an alien, but it had escaped. I didn't like them much.

Then Foo whispers, 'You ready, Kylie? Tommo?'

'Something's not right,' Kylie says.

But Foo says, '*Shh*,' and we go quiet again.

*

A few minutes later, and Kylie and I are 402 years in the future, without any obvious way of getting back.

The monkey, it turns out, was just the start of it.

CHAPTER 20

'Before we meet our next guests,' says Des, 'let's have a quick look at how it all started.'

On the TV monitors suspended from the high studio ceiling a film starts with pictures that were taken by a TV crew that came to our house a few days ago. There's Kylie and me at home with Mam, and pictures of our school and the IT Club with Mrs Dundas, not that they had much to do with it.

A voice on the film – Andy's, I think – starts.

'*Meet our latest master and mistress of mystery, cousins Thomas Reeve and Kylie Woollagong from Culvercot on the glorious north-east coast just downriver from our studios here in Newcastle. We love a bit of time travel at the Ministry of Mystery so we sent our cameras along to find out if Kylie and Thomas really are gonna go back to the future!*'

The film isn't long. When it's finished, Andy looks into a camera and reads the words on the autocue.

'Well! I really don't know what to make of that! An iPad that can connect you to the future – *or so it's claimed*!' He gives a cheeky smile as the studio audience cheers at hearing the show's catchphrase. 'Shall we meet them, Des? Aye, why not, or they'd have wasted their bus fare to get here . . .' (We were picked up in a swanky Mercedes this afternoon. It's just one of his jokes.)

Des says, 'Give it up for our would-be Tyneside Time Lords – Kylie and her cousin Tommo!'

The *Doctor Who* music plays, and the audience whoops and cheers. Foo whispers, 'Off you go! Break a leg!' and gives me a gentle push in the back. In a kind of daze, I find myself walking across the vinyl planks towards the big blue sofa where Andy and Des are standing and applauding.

The studio audience is clapping too, and I glance out at them. The bright lights make it difficult to see anything, but I can make out Mam and Dad in the front row whooping loudly.

'Take a seat, Thomas. Welcome to the Ministry of Mystery. Make yourself comfortable.' This is Des speaking. He's got a very friendly voice, and I begin to feel less scared straight away. 'That is one *heck* of a story, Kylie! Can you understand why some people – not us, oh no, but *some* people – might think you're tellin' so many lies that it's a wonder your pants have not set fire to our sofa!'

Audience laughter, and I laugh along too. We did this in the mini-rehearsal earlier. Kylie gives the answer we'd practised. 'I know. It seems unbelievable, doesn't it?'

'Sure does, but that's the nature of the Ministry of Mystery,' says Andy. 'You claim, Kylie Woollagong, that your tablet computer will connect to a civilisation four hundred years in the future and that all you have to do is turn it on and we'll see everything on the tablet screen, is that right?'

'That's right,' Kylie says, but I can hear a murmur of something – disbelief, perhaps – pass through the audience.

'All right. Well, we'll see a demo later, and, hand on heart, this could be the most incredible thing ever to happen on television anywhere! Or perhaps not, of course. But first of all, Thomas: what's it like having a megabrained cousin?'

I grin. 'It's handy when it comes to homework!'

The audience laughs, even though this was another scripted line suggested to me by Des earlier. I don't really mind, I'm having fun, but I still think something's up with Kylie. She's tense and keeps looking at the Time Tablet that she's put down on a glass-topped table in front of the sofa. There's also the yew sapling to the side and the metal Time Trapper canister.

'So – here it is, the device in question,' says Andy. 'What's going to happen, Kylie? What's this baby tree for?'

'Well, when we finish this programme, the Time Tablet's going to go into this capsule here, which I will bury in our back garden with this tree as a marker.'

'And you're hoping that enough people will know

about it, thanks to this programme, that someone in four hundred and two years' time will dig it up – is that right?' says Andy.

'That's right. I'll make a metal plaque to put in the ground next to the tree that will last forever. Assuming someone finds it . . .'

'That's a big old assumption if you don't mind me saying,' says Des, raising an eyebrow to the audience, who chuckle.

'Yeah, but still – it's a big old tree!' says Kylie, unbothered by this teasing. She gets a laugh. 'When it's found, the Time Tablet will connect with Permasat, and the solar storm will allow us to communicate!'

Andy is grinning broadly. 'As simple as that, eh? Well, let's hope that in the year 2425 –' he checks his watch – 'one minute from now, someone has found your Time Tablet and is waiting to speak to us from . . . the future. Do you wanna see that, everyone?'

The audience roars its approval, and under the noise I hear Kylie say, 'Oh crikey, Tommo – it's not gonna work.'

CHAPTER 21

OCEAN

Word has got around. In fact, enough people know about our 'Bowled Experiment In Tyme' that by 7.30 p.m. there must be more than a hundred people inside the crumbling walls of the roofless old church in Culvercot, 'cluding Sunbeam, her mam and dad and all six of her bros.

Nanny Moo has said she 'cannit be bothered with all that nonsense, not with four crates of crab to prep', which I was a bit hurt about at first, but it is all right. There will, I can admit to myself, be nothing to see.

One of the first to arrive, to our surprise, is Frau Schwartz from the library. She sits in the middle of the front row of pews, straight-backed, hands clasped in her lap, staring ahead and looking disapproving.

Duke paces up and down, muttering and gesturing as he rehearses his words. Monsieur Lumière sits at the side, his arm still in a sling. His head bandage has been removed and he has repaired his wig so, along with his recoloured and rewaxed facial hair, he looks more or less back to normal. The only thing missing is Pierre by his side in a matching jacket.

Suddenly Duke stops, and I see that he is looking at the crowd of people, and chewing his bottom lip.

'What are you thinking?' I ask him, and his head snaps round like I have woken him from a bad dream.

'When I was at sea,' he says, his voice a little hesitant, 'I . . . I always used to get a sense of when a storm was approaching. The crew nicknamed me "storm boy". I was seldom mistook.'

I look up at the sky through the missing roof of the church. There were indeed storm clouds building in the south.

'I don't mean that,' he says. 'Anyone can see storm clouds. I mean . . . summink else.' He blinks rapidly while he stares at me.

'Stop it, Duke. You are fearifying me.'

He does not stop. 'Do you fink, four hundred and two years in the past, they're preparing to talk to us? Because, if this is gonna work, then that is what's happening. Somewhere near here on this day, Kylie and Thomas are waiting to look at the future. I can feel it, like I can feel the weather.'

A voice calls out from the small crowd. 'Oi! Frenchie! You startin' or what? It's gonna rain any minute!' Then a slow handclap starts.

'Quickly, Ocean!' hisses Monsieur Lumière. '*La musique!*'

I crank the handle of the gramophone and place the needle on the spinning disc. 'Mediately, the music starts to come from the brass horn and the words of the song 'Rock Around the Clock' fill the space.

Duke has put on his best lilac tailcoat and grey gloves. He looks like Monsieur Lumière in miniature. He has even coloured his pale eyebrows dark with burnt cork. He adjusts his hat, clears his throat and steps forward to a spot in the centre of the church. I lift the needle off the disc, and the music stops abruptly, making everyone look up.

'Lays and gennlemen! *Mesdames et messieurs*. Boys and girls! It is a great honour to be back here among you . . .'

'You gonna set fire to the place like your uncle did, son?' comes a shouted voice, and there is a ripple of chuckles. Duke smiles, although I can tell he is not very amused.

He continues. 'Tonight, everybody, we have the chance to witness a global first! Summink never before seen in the history of the uff!'

'The what?' shouts a boy who I know from school.

'The uff. The uff! The planet we live on! And you, my friends, will be the ones to see it. As Monsieur Lumière has promised, if this does not work, then all your money will be refunded . . .'

'What about *Star Wars* then?' shouts the same boy.

Poor Duke. He is not used to this. Monsieur Lumière

would cover the interruptions with a joke, but I can tell Duke is upset. 'What do you mean, *Star Wars*?'

'At the Fish Fair. I paid to see *Star Wars*, and I never saw the end of it, did I? What happened to Luke Whatsisname? Did he blow up the Death Star or not? I want my money back for that!'

The crowd are laughing openly now, but Duke struggles on, trying to keep the wobble from his voice.

'Ha ha, my friend! I . . . I promise you – after tonight's spectacu-lacular hexhibition, you will be more than satisfied. For I present to you, my friend, to you all . . .'

He pauses for dramatic effect, and I am pleased that he has regained control.

'The Time Tablet!'

As he had instructed, I walk out from the side, holding the Time Tablet in the air as a fat drop of rain falls on the dusty ground at my feet.

No one applauds, so Duke carries on speaking as Monsieur Lumière beams with delight. 'Four hundred and two years ago, at this very time, an attempt was made to communicate with the future. With now! And so, as we count down to precisely eight p.m., we will find out if it's possible to see the Wonder Age on this screen!'

'Is that it?' says the same boy. 'It's gotta be a fake!'

'Ocean: the switch if you please!'

And now a number of things happen in the next half

a minute, starting with a gentle roll of thunder coming from the south and more heavy raindrops.

Suddenly there is a whistling above my head and a loud *thwack* from behind me. The crowd gasps. I turn to see the bolt from a crossbow embedded in the old stone pulpit at my back. There is a scream from the audience as, at the rear of the church, four men on horseback appear through the ruined doorway. One holds a crossbow; another points a large shotgun straight up in the air and fires.

Seconds later, the tiny pellets from the shotgun cartridge join the rain peppering the ground. Everyone has turned to look as the leader, a large bearded man with an overhanging belly, walks his white horse to the end of the aisle. He lowers the crossbow and points it straight at us. The crowd are silent.

'Move your hand away from that device, little girl, or face the consequences,' he says, quietly at first before raising his voice. 'You 'eard me, Deucalion! Tell 'er. Don't make me ask twice.'

I look over at Duke, who has turned grey. 'Pinker!' he gasps.

CHAPTER 22

The bearded man walks his white horse nearer to us. He is followed by another man whose horse is a deep auburn and who is holding on to something behind him. The two remaining horsemen stay at the back.

Pinker stops a few metres from us, but does not dismount. He is every bit as ugly as Duke told me. His greasy grey-streaked hair is pulled back into a ponytail, and his face and neck are covered with livid, sore-looking boils. He grins a snaggle-toothed grimace and spits on the ground.

'Hello, Deucalion,' he snarls. 'Bin a while, eh? My, how you've grown.' He turns his head to Monsieur Lumière. 'An' my bruvver-in-law an' all! Well, well, well. Ain't that nice? A family reunion. Looks like I arrived just in time. You don't look well, Lumière. Wh'appened?'

Monsieur Lumière is on his feet. 'What do you want, Pinker?'

Pinker manoeuvres his horse so that he is side-on to the crowd and they can hear him.

'Only what's rightly mine, you French fraud. That

device belongs to me an' you know it. You cheated at cards, you wretch. Meanwhile, this little *gaunerschlingel* 'ere –' he waves the crossbow casually towards Duke, making him duck – 'stole the newspaper that indicated where this device would be found. *Didn't you?* Duke flinches but says nothing.

'You beast, Pinker,' growls Monsieur Lumière. 'You mistreated this boy for years. You expect fairness in return?'

'Nope. Just the Time Tablet. 'And it over.'

Monsieur Lumière glances at me. 'Quickly, Ocean. Press the "on" button. It is time.'

So I do and, well . . .

Everything changes.

In my hands, the Time Tablet's screen is now illuminated a milky-white, its surface appearing to ripple.

'Oh my Lord,' says Duke. 'Are you doing that?'

'I have not done anything,' I croak. 'It is doing it by itself.'

I place it on the floor, and step back.

''And it over!' bellows Pinker, standing up in the stirrups. 'Or perhaps my new little friend should persuade you?' He waves his hand at the man on the auburn horse, who reaches behind him and unties something. Seconds later, Pierre is on the ground, running towards Monsieur Lumière, squeaking with joy, his little arms spread wide.

'Pierre! *Oh, mon petit ami!*' Monsieur Lumière sinks to one knee and opens his arms.

Pierre is within a metre of him when he is jerked back harshly by a long rope attached to the leather collar round his neck. The rider on the auburn horse cackles cruelly and pulls harder on the rope, making Pierre squeal.

'I 'eard all about your fire, Lumière. Such a shame. 'Course I know everythin' about losin' your life's work in a disaster. Still – you should take better care of your animal. Scared out of 'is wits, 'e was – ran for 'is life. I found 'im half dead by the old Tyne Bridge, din't I? Massive clue, 'e was. I knew then that my hunch was right: that you'd come 'ere to find the Time Tablet. He led me straight to you. 'Im an' the posters you've put up everywhere. Most 'elpful.'

And now he turns his horse till he faces the audience, and he lowers the crossbow to his side. 'Don't be afraid, folks. You're in no danger from me. Only from this liar, cheat and fraudster behind me. 'E's already destroyed an 'istoric building with 'is recklessness, brought these two innocent children under 'is evil spell *and* spent years mistreating this poor monkey!'

'For *shame,*' tuts Frau Schwartz in the front row.

'It ain't true!' cries Duke.

'Lies!' shouts Monsieur Lumière.

There is a rumbling in the crowd that I do not like the sound of. But it is instantly drowned out by a shout of alarm from the man on the auburn horse. Pierre, in one swift movement, has leaped on to the horse's back and sunk his sharp teeth into the animal's flank. The horse whinnies in pain and rears up while its rider lets go of the long leash attached to Pierre's collar in order to tighten the horse's reins.

The Time Tablet is still glowing on the floor before me, its light almost blinding. As the horse rears up, Pierre clings on tightly to the saddle, trying to regain his balance. Then I watch in silent horror as, in a single movement, Pierre falls from the back of the bucking horse straight *into* the rectangle of light.

It is as though the Time Tablet swallows him up.

In a second, he has gone, *sucked into the screen!*

I cannot believe my eyes. I look around desperately. Has anyone else seen this?

'No, no, no . . . Pierre!' I cry, and I rush forward.

The tablet is still glowing white, and I fall to my knees, gazing into the glowing screen. Maybe I had been mistaken? Where is he? The rope that was attached to Pierre is now disappearing into the Time Tablet, and I quickly wrap my hand round the end.

The audience has left the wooden benches, surging towards us for a better view and blocking Pinker from advancing with his horse. 'Get outta the way!' he shouts, but he is ignored.

'Did you see that?' someone says.

'That monkey just disappeared!'

'It is EEFIL! It is the work of SATAN!' screeches Frau Schwartz.

Duke steps forward. 'What happened? Where's he gone? Did he . . .'

'He is in there!' I scream, pointing at the tablet. My hand, with the rope now wrapped round it, is being pulled towards the screen. My fist goes straight into the milky-white surface, and I try to yank it back, terrified. Then, as another crack of thunder makes the few remaining glass panes in the church windows tremble and the sky light up with electricity, I grit my teeth and plunge my whole arm into the screen and feel Pierre's damp little hand gripping my first two fingers with surprising force.

I am being pulled towards the screen by a monkey that I cannot even see. Then I lose my grip, and I am left with my arm up to my shoulder in the tablet.

Around me, people are gasping with horror, and Pinker is screaming, 'Look! I told you! I told you!' But even he has stopped his advance, stunned into stoppingness by the 'straordinary sight before his eyes.

Doc Mason shouts, 'Will everybody just calm down! It's an illusion, no more. Lumière is a showman – what do you expect?'

This seems to quieten people, although I am still frantically reaching into nothing for the monkey's paw.

Doc Mason continues. 'Do you not see? It must be some sort of trick with mirrors or a trapdoor! Frightfully effective!'

'Oh really, Doc?' sneers another voice. 'So where are the mirrors then? Look at her arm, man!'

Monsieur Lumière is next to me, hissing, 'What is happening, Ocean?'

The rain is coming more heavily now, and splattering on the cracked tiled floor of the church.

'Grab it!' screams Pinker. He eases his bulksome frame from the saddle and lands heavily. 'Stop it 'appening or you're all doomed! If this goes any further, this whole world will end in an instant.'

What can he mean?

Frau Schwartz cries, 'I tolt you – it is eefil!'

For a few seconds, I am trapped: my arm is in one century, the rest of me in another. Pinker steps forward, shoving people aside.

'*Help me!*' I shout.

CHAPTER 23

THOMAS

Andy is still looking at his watch. 'All right, everybody,' he says. 'It's comin' up to the time Kylie and Tommo have been waitin' for. Will we see the future? Let's find out in ten, nine, eight . . .'

Everyone joins in the countdown. 'Seven, six, five, four, three, two, one . . .'

Nothing happens.

The audience goes quiet, and then they start to laugh. And after they've laughed, and still nothing has happened, they start to jeer. It's good-natured jeering, but it's still a *little bit* hostile. Andy and Des are on it at once.

'Hey, hey, hey! Give 'em a chance! Give 'em a chance! You're not at St James's Park now!' This is Andy speaking. He's on his feet, talking to the audience, sort of mock-serious.

I'm thinking, *Thanks, Andy.* He's good at this. He manages to calm the audience down – even *tell them off* – while still making them laugh with a reference to

Newcastle United's home ground. 'Where did we get this lot from?' he jokes to Des, and the audience cheers and roars with laughter.

Calm has been restored.

'It's all right, everybody,' says Andy. 'We like to have an answer here on the Ministry of Mystery, don't we, Des?'

'Oh aye. Because we have the ultimate Time Lord with us here today! Yes, *Doctor Who* has been running on BBC television since 1963. You'll remember it well, Andy!'

'Like yesterday,' laughs Andy as the studio lights dim a little, and the familiar sound of the *Doctor Who* theme tune fades up.

Diddly-dum, diddly-dum, diddly-dum, diddly-dum . . .

But not for long because, at that moment, something moving on the screen of the Time Tablet catches my eye.

'Ee, my word, something's happenin',' says Des, pointing at the screen.

One of the cameras moves a bit closer. Kylie and I lean in for a better look, and Kylie nudges me. The screen has changed colour and, instead of a reflective black, it's now a sort of bright milky-grey, and the surface appears to be rippling like a tiny pond on a windy day.

Kylie catches my eye. 'Is that meant to happen?' I whisper to her, forgetting that I'm wearing a microphone clipped to my shirt collar. My comment is amplified to the audience, who laugh again.

'No flippin' idea, mate. It . . . it . . .'

Whatever she was going to say stays in her mouth because suddenly there's a scream from the audience as a tiny hairy human hand pushes up through the rippling screen.

'Whoa! Check it out! That's amazin'!' gasps Andy.

Des peers even closer, his nose centimetres from the screen. 'What's going on? I've no idea, people, but this is unplanned and unbelievable!'

The audience starts to whoop and applaud, and then suddenly, as though propelled by some force within the tablet, a long streak of brown and purple shoots out of the screen, hovers for half a second at our eye level before gravity pulls it back to the table and it re-forms into . . .

'A live monkey just came out of the tablet, Tommo,' murmurs Kylie.

I can hardly hear her because the studio audience is screaming with, well . . . what? Horror? Delight? Fear? Probably all of them. Unable to tear my eyes away from what's happening, I say, 'I can see that, Kylie. Is that, you know, meant to happen?'

'Uh-uh.'

The monkey's hairy little head is swivelling, and its teeth are bared in a look of perplexed terror. Then I look across at Kylie, and her expression is exactly the same.

The noise of the studio audience has become a dull roar in my head.

'This is just awesome. Gerra look at that!' shouts Andy directly to the camera, grinning like mad and pointing at the monkey, who is wearing a little purple jacket. 'It's a flippin' monkey!'

I squint my eyes, trying to see beyond the bright lights to the front row of the studio audience where Mam and Dad are sitting. I can make out their shapes, and Dad looks like he's shrugging his shoulders at Mam in a *I have no idea, either* sort of gesture.

The whole studio is going
ABSOLUTELY
CRAZY.

People are on their feet, cheering and clapping, and, to be honest, it's hard to blame them. Because to them this is the most awesome magic trick ever. Andy and Des are on their feet too, applauding and shaking their heads in disbelief.

Under the noise of the audience, Des says to me and Kylie, 'Did you two plan this all along? You cheeky so-and-sos! I have *no idea* how you did it!'

Andy makes the audience laugh by looking under the low table as though there might be a secret compartment where we hid the monkey while, off-camera, Foo the studio assistant is frantically signalling something to Des.

The poor terrified-looking animal swivels its head again, fixing its gaze on Kylie. Then, in one movement, it leaps at her, clambering on to her upper arm, pulling on her neck to regain its balance, and finally perching on her shoulder like a pirate's parrot, where it starts to rummage through her hair, looking for bugs. It's then that I notice the cord attached to the monkey's collar. It's taut and goes straight back into the screen.

Kylie starts to scream, but then freezes in terror, which the audience finds even funnier. Des is doubled over with laughter, and Andy is wiping his eyes, unable to speak. I'm in the middle of it all, staring at the tablet. The screen has started to wobble again. Behind us, the door of Doctor Who's TARDIS opens, and a man pops his head out.

'Er, hello? Is it my bit now?'

Everyone ignores him because of the noise and commotion around us. Andy has got his breath back enough to address the camera.

'Well, that's the Ministry of Mystery for you, folks! You never know what's gonna happen next. I tell you – no one was expecting *that*! Hang on – there's another one coming!'

He points to the tablet where a hand, a human one this time, has emerged from the screen.

'Whoa!' gasps Des. 'The mysteries just keep on comin'!'

The left hand emerging from the screen is joined by a matching right hand, and the monkey clambers down from Kylie's shoulder towards them. Then she starts going, '*Ow, ow, ow!*' because the monkey's hand is tangled in her mass of corkscrew curls and her glasses.

The two hands grasp the monkey's outstretched paw and pull hard, forcing Kylie to lean forward, still yelping as her hair is pulled.

In the next instant, a horrified silence descends on the scene. This isn't funny any more, and the audience in the TV studio can tell, as can Andy and Des, who stare in grim fascination. Kylie is being pulled nearer and nearer to the tablet. I think everyone believes this is meant to happen – that it's all part of the big illusion. But it isn't. Not at all: I can tell from Kylie's terrified face as she is pulled nearer the tablet.

'Thomas! Tommo!' she cries, stretching out her hand to me.

Then, just like watching a cartoon where a big dog squeezes through a tiny catflap, Kylie's head and shoulders are sucked into the screen of the iPad. Such is her terror, she has my wrist in a hard, painful grip.

'Pull, Thomas, pu—' But then her head and shoulders are gone, and I'm being dragged in as well. The last thing I see is a look of delighted amazement, mixed with baffled terror, on the face of Britain's most popular TV hosts as, live on television, with a sort of rushing in my ears, and the sensation of being stretched like a rubber band, I'm pulled into the tablet's screen.

The last thing I hear is my mam's scream of, '*Thomaaaas!*'

CHAPTER 24

The sound of the studio audience's screaming is still ringing in my head.

I can still hear Andy saying, 'Ha ha! That's one impressive illusion!'

Still feel the weird sensation of being pulled into a screen by my cousin. And a monkey . . .

Did I just say 'weird'? Sorry, but 'weird' doesn't even *begin* to describe something that didn't happen, surely. It can't have happened. Things like that just *don't* happen. Perhaps I'm dreaming?

I turn to see a girl in a smock and red wellington boots hovering by the Time Tablet. Our eyes meet, and she mouths *Thomas* before she's yanked into the pool of light from the screen.

A voice I don't recognise shouts, 'Ocean! Come back!'

It's like the aftershock of a massive explosion; my skin is tingling all over, and I feel as though I'm going to throw up. Then, slowly, my eyes regain focus, my vision stops swimming, and I hear a voice.

'What in the name of Jiminy Cricket's going on? Is

that you, Tommo? Whoa! Where are we? Who are these people? Ow, ow, ow! I've got something in my hair? *Gaaaah!* What is it? Ohmigod, it's that blimmin' monkey! Get off, you little pest!'

I'm looking around, blinking hard and completely terrified. Although I'm no expert in reading the facial expressions of monkeys, I could swear it's looking at me in confusion and fear, and I can hardly blame it for that's what I'm feeling as well.

Suddenly the monkey leaps away as I stagger back. For a moment – less than that, a *second* – I see it land on top of the Time Tablet, which is now on the ground and still glowing white. And then, where the monkey was . . . it just isn't any more. It's as though it is drawn back into the screen like some sort of special effect. The cord attached to its neck disappears too, sucked in like a strand of spaghetti.

Is that what happened to us?

As I reel backwards, Kylie catches me in her strong arms, and we stay there, holding each other, as we look round the big space and the crowd of people who are staring at us in near-silent astonishment.

The studio roof, with all its lights and monitors – everything – has gone. In fact, the whole set has disappeared. It's been replaced by what looks like a half-ruined building in the shape of an old church, with half a roof and half a surviving stained-glass window at the end, and the walls almost completely demolished. Andy and Des are nowhere to be seen. The cameras, the lights, the studio audience, the shiny floor – all are gone. And it's raining.

I wriggle free of Kylie's grasp and shout, 'Mam? Mam?' It's the first thing I think of. Then, 'Dad?'

I scan the crowd of people, desperately searching for a familiar face. They don't seem remotely amused by whatever's just happened. They look horrified. Next to Kylie and me is a man in a purple coat. He's picked up the Time Tablet and is shaking it, yelling at it. 'Ocean! Ocean! Pierre!' he shouts, for some reason. His shaking dislodges a photograph that was affixed to the back and it drops to the floor, unnoticed. Nearby, a man standing next to a white horse is pointing a shaking finger at him and growling, 'Look what you did – you pathetic worm, Lumière!' And it over now before you do any more damage.'

From the crowd comes a squealing voice, 'It's eefil, I tell you,' and someone else shouts, 'Oh, give it a rest, Schwartz. It's a trick!'

'Kylie? What's happening? Where's Mam?' I'm clinging on to my cousin's arm, suddenly glad that she's so big.

She looks completely dazed and doesn't meet my eye. 'I have absolutely no flippin' idea, mate.'

My eye is drawn to a scuffle in the front row of the crowd. The man with the horse has stepped forward aggressively, and one or two others are making a poor attempt at holding him back.

A man says, 'Leave it out, pal. They're just kids. It's an illusion!'

The horseman pushes the man aside and stomps to within a few metres of us, pointing a stubby finger as he bellows, 'It's dangerous. I told you, did I not? This is definitely evil!'

'Jiminy, Tommo, I think he means us.'

Everyone else is in costume – every single one dressed in a combination of patched and dirty old clothes.

'Mam? Dad?' I shout again.

'Who are these people?' murmurs Kylie. 'It's like a charity-shop convention.'

The man in the purple coat has raised his hands and is shouting above the clamour, 'Ladies, gentlemen. Calm down, please. I can explain everything. Pinker – I am sure we can come to an arrangement.'

'This 'ad better be good, Lumière!' snarls the big man. 'Where did those kids come from? I'm going nowhere, an' when I'm ready I'll just take the tablet an' be off. You know you won't be able to stop me so . . . take your time, *mon ami*.' He folds his arms in mock patience, and I already know that I hate him.

'It . . . it is all quite safe,' stammers the man called Lumière, although his nervous glances at Kylie and me suggest he's exaggerating at least a bit. I certainly don't feel safe.

I look around desperately and see a plump elderly

lady in spectacles clamber up on to one of the wooden benches and scream, 'This is witchcraft! Lumière – what have you done with little Ocean? You are an eefil influence, a malign presence! Listen to me, everybody! You all know me from ze library, and I say this is the work of Satan himself – and in a holy place too. They must be stopped!'

I can tell that the crowd is getting angry. This woman shouting about witchcraft has turned the mood very ugly indeed.

Then a boy in a bowler hat and a long coat comes forward from the side of the platform we're on. He's quite possibly the skinniest boy I have ever seen, with a wide slice of a mouth and bony hands like chicken's feet. I recoil, and I hear myself squeak with fear.

'Was this meant to happen . . . *Kylie?*'

I sense Kylie tense up behind me. 'I . . . I dunno. How do you know my name?'

I open my mouth, but no sound will come out, even though all I want to do is say, 'Kylie?'

It comes out as '*K . . . K . . .*'

I feel my cousin's hand on my shoulder. 'You all right, Tommo?'

'No.'

'It's okay. Me neither.' And the hand squeezes. The fat man, fed up of waiting, is now getting on his horse, and, in the few seconds that he struggles to position his bulk in the saddle and settle the animal, the boy hisses at us.

'Listen to me.' He glances at the horse guy, who has a sneer all over his lumpy face. 'We have to get outta here. We're not safe. They'll follow us.'

His single good eye catches the light and stares at us, frightened.

'*Follow us?*' I say. 'Who's going to follow us? Where's Andy and Des? Where's my mam?'

'Just *trust me!*'

The guy on the horse makes it rear up threateningly. 'That's it!' he screams. 'I've 'ad enough. You've 'ad your fun. Now 'and it over.' He raises the crossbow to his shoulder and pulls back the bolt.

CHAPTER 25

The man – Lumière – holds up both hands in surrender, and the crossbow is slowly lowered. He addresses the crowd. 'There is an explan-iation for everything if you would only calm down. First, though, I need to refund your money. Here – catch!'

He reaches into a plastic bag at his side and brings out a handful of coins that he throws to the crowd. The heavy coins hit people on the head as they rain down. Several of them go, 'Ow!' and they start to shout.

'Are you mad, Lumière?'

'What did you do that for?'

'That did not work as I planned,' says Lumière to us. 'There is only one thing left to do.'

'What's that?' says Kylie.

'Run! Run to the Wonderbuggy – now! Follow me!'

'Stop them!' yells Pinker. 'Fifty crowns for anyone bringing me the Time Tablet!'

And so – without understanding anything – we run because it's the only suggestion anyone has made. I honestly think I would have followed anybody who sounded as though they knew what they were doing.

We have a few seconds' start, but a few people in the crowd have obviously decided that fifty crowns is a prize worth pursuing us for. Kylie grabs the Time Tablet and, stumbling, we follow Lumière out of the crooked wooden door at the back, and he slams it shut, but it will only delay our pursuers by a second or two. Besides, there's a section of broken wall a little further down, and two people are already climbing through that.

'Outta the way, you idiots!' shouts Pinker. I glance back and see that he's aiming his crossbow at us. 'I can't get a clean shot!' A second later, a bolt whooshes over my head and smashes one of the church windows, sending broken glass flying.

Directly ahead of us is a . . .

Okay. I don't know what the heck it is. It's shaped vaguely like a tractor; it has big wheels, and that, at the moment, seems like a good thing. There's a pipe coming out of the top, belching thick fumes, but now is not the time for a detailed description because the small crowd is gaining on us, and I can see somebody else mounting a horse.

'Get on, get on!' shouts Lumière. 'Duke – out of the seat!'

The skinny kid leaps to one side as Lumière takes his place at the exact moment that Kylie and I grab hold of what looks like a car door. She's hanging on with one hand, while gripping the Time Tablet in the other.

Behind us, a small child is running as fast as a small child can, and he's obviously determined to grab the Time Tablet. Kylie hasn't seen this, and as we pick up speed in the vehicle I scream at her, 'Kylie – look out!'

The child's hands are millimetres away from contact with the Time Tablet when Kylie glances down and aims her shiny Doc Marten boot right in the poor kid's chest. With a yelp of, '*Urk!*', he goes flying into a thorny bush, forcing another grown-up pursuer to stop and help him.

The vehicle is picking up speed, bouncing violently along a cracked and potholed road on its massive worn tractor tyres. Every couple of metres, another part of it comes loose and falls off: a handle here, a panel there. The vehicle is breaking up beneath us. Two more crossbow bolts slam into the rear of the tractor, *thunk! thunk!*

My hands are aching with the effort of hanging on. More than once, I think I'm going to be thrown clear, or pulled beneath the big tractor wheels. And then I look behind.

'Faster!' I shout. 'Two horses are gaining on us!'

The skinny kid leaps out of the seat at the front and squeezes past me into the interior of the tractor cabin. He emerges seconds later, clutching a plastic box.

'Hang on to me!' he yells. He pushes his bowler hat down firmly on to his head and climbs to the top of the creaking vehicle. 'Hold my belt!'

He edges further back, the box in one hand. I reach up and wrap my fingers into the belt holding up his trousers. I don't know what good I'm doing: if he comes off now, he'll probably drag me with him.

The horses are nearly level with us now, and one of the riders, a young man, has released his reins and taken out a shotgun, which he aims at the tractor's fat tyres.

'Whatever you're going to do,' I shout, 'you'd better do it *right now*!'

I can see the rider's finger tightening on the trigger.

The boy leans even further out and, in a single movement, upends the box, spilling thousands of large nails on to the road behind us and right into the path of the oncoming horses. With loud whinnies, both animals rear up as the nails prick their hooves, tossing their riders out of the saddle and sending them crashing to the ground. There's a loud bang as the shotgun discharges towards the pursuing crowd, who scream and duck.

'Wha-hey!' I cheer. 'We've done it!'

'No, we haven't!' shouts Kylie. She's looking ahead with a terrified expression. 'We're running out of road.'

Sure enough, in about fifty metres, the road is blocked by a massive fallen tree, and we're heading straight for it.

CHAPTER 26

OCEAN

The sensation of falling through a small screen is very 'culiar. I am not sure I can say much more because it was over so soon that it did not 'zactly hurt. There is nothing that I can compare it with. Perhaps it is what flying in an aerialplane feels like; I would not know.

Pierre went first – he just seemed to fall into the light from the Time Tablet. I tried to stop him. I really did.

'What the blazes just happened?' I hear somebody shout, a voice rising above a loud crowd of people.

'Where's the rest of them?'

'Who the heck's she?'

'That's a real monkey – it's not a puppet!'

Pierre and I are in a room with a huge window, blinding white lights and so many people making so much noise. I blink several times and look around: Monsieur Lumière, Thomas, Kylie, Duke . . . they are nowhere to be seen. The man on the white horse that Duke had said was Pinker has gone too. Everything is different.

This was surely not meant to happen. I thought we would simply be looking at pictures sent from the Wonder Age. Perhaps talking to the people in them? If it worked at all, that is. That would have been 'mazing enough. I cannot think clearly, though, for all the lights, the people and the shouting.

'Who are you, pet?'

'Where've you come from?'

'Andy – did you set this up?'

'What's your name? Where's Thomas?'

'Where is Kylie?'

'Where's the monkey from, love?'

Behind me, a man is standing in the doorway of a huge blue box with little windows and a light on top, yelling, 'Will somebody tell me just what on earth is going on?'

Shouts, yells, questions, more shouts . . .

There must be a hundred, no two hundred, people in the vast room, some buzzing round me with curly wires coming from their ears and many, many more on seats like an old-style cinema or theatre. Some are applauding; some are cheering; many are holding hand-sized rectangular things in front of them. (I think these must be cellphones. If this is the Wonder Age that is. I am still not sure.)

There are two men in suits who seem vaguely familiar. One of them touches his ear and mutters, 'Right . . . right . . . okay,' then he says something to the other man, and they both turn to a box with a lens attached (a camera, I suppose).

'Ee, I tell you, folks, it's crazy here, isn't it, Des?'

'Ha ha! But all under control, of course. Oh yes! That's it for this incredible edition of the *Ministry of Mystery*! Comin' up next on BBC 1, it's *Passion Palace*. See you next time!'

The two men hold their smiles and then, after a few seconds, their faces show a mixture of confusion and concern. The shorter one yells, 'Are we off air, Celia? Right – will someone tell us just what's goin' on? Who is this girl? Is someone lookin' after her? Where are the two kids we were talkin' to?'

If I had thought before that it was chaos, what happens next is even worse. I am standing in the middle of it all, holding Pierre tight, and all I want is my Nanny Moo.

'Andy . . . Andy, man! Did you know about this?' says one and that is when I realise who they are.

'Of course not, mate. Not a clue. It's gotta be some sort of set-up? Someone getting revenge for one of our pranks!'

Des approaches and puts a gentle arm on my shoulder. 'Hey, pet, are you all right? Can you tell us what's happenin'?'

He is pushed aside by a blonde woman in a T-shirt and headphones. 'Let me handle this, Desmond. Now, sweetheart – where have you come from? Where did you get the monkey? Who set this up?'

Des narrows his eyes and says, 'Celia – can't you see she's scared? Tell security to get the audience out of here right now.'

The blonde lady gives this a moment's thought, then bellows, 'All right, everybody, the show's over! Make your way to the exits, please!'

Everywhere I look, people are shouting at me, flashing their cameras at me, while three men in uniform try in vain to stop the crowd getting closer. I look down at the Time Tablet on the floor, hoping with all my heart that the screen is still rippling milky-white, because right now anything at all would be preferable to this. I pick it up, but the screen is black even when I tap it. Then I hear a woman's voice – loud, desperate and very angry.

'*Stop!*'

The crowd goes quiet as a woman in jeans and a silky blouse pushes to the front of them.

'Are you all mad? Can't you see this is a frightened girl? Back off. Back off now!'

'Just doin' w'job, pet. Publicity, you know?' This is said by a man with two cameras and sweat stains on his shirt. But he lowers his camera.

She turns to me and crouches down on one knee so that she is actually looking up into my face. She studies me carefully. Still the flashes continue and the *ksssk* noises. The woman looks behind her and snarls, 'I swear, the next person to take a picture will find their camera halfway down their throat.'

It seems to work. In the hush that follows, she turns her head to me and talks so slowly and gently that I find tears pricking my eyes.

'My name is Melissa. I'm Thomas's mam, and Kylie's aunty. What's your name, honey?'

I tell her. The woman swallows hard as if holding back tears. 'That's a nice name. Have you seen Thomas?'

I nod – even though it was only for a second.

'Oh my word,' she breathes. 'Where is he? And Kylie?'

'I do not know.'

'All right. And is he . . . alive? Is he okay?'

I nod again. 'I think so.'

'Thank God for that.'

She hugs me tight, and I find myself hugging her back and sobbing with relief that somebody wants me to be safe. A man has joined us and kneels next to Melissa and me.

'I'm Thomas's dad,' he says. 'Can you tell us where Thomas and Kylie are?'

I look round the room. 'They are . . . they were right next to me. Right there, in fact.' I point about two metres away where a man is talking into a little box attached to his jacket. 'And . . . and a man on a horse fired a . . . a thing at me and he wanted it.'

Thomas's parents exchange looks, and I cannot tell if they are pleased with what I have told them or not.

Thomas's dad says, 'Can we . . . can you bring Thomas back? And Kylie?' He picks up the Time Tablet from the floor and looks at it carefully.

'I . . . I do not know,' I say, wiping my eyes on my wrist. 'I do not know how it works. We . . . we do not have things like this where I live.'

'It's all right, pet. We don't have them here, either,' says Melissa. Her voice is trembling and so quiet that I have to strain to hear it. 'At least . . . we didn't. Right now, though, we need you to be very brave and very honest and tell us everything you know, all right? We'll get rid of all these people, and we'll see if we can put this right, okay?'

I nod.

'What is your monkey called, sweetheart?' says Thomas's dad.

'Pierre,' I say.

'Really? A French name! *Bonjour*, Pierre,' he says. He holds out his hand to Pierre, who takes it. '*Je m'appelle Freddie*,' and it makes a few people laugh, and even I sort of snuffle-laugh, and it all makes the whole fury and tension in the room pop like a balloon. A few flashes go off, but it does not really matter any more. Melissa hugs me tight, and I feel her chest shaking as she sobs, while all around us the shouting and chaos continue.

A few minutes pass like that. I hear someone mention, 'Police are here.' Melissa and Freddie stand up and beckon over a woman who might be a policer for a hushly conversation that I do not really hear much of.

The policer clears her throat. 'Right, everybody. That's it for now. The girl and the monkey are staying here for the moment. Thomas's parents have requested that we ask you to leave and will not be granting interviews at this time. Kindly make your way to the exits in an orderly manner, thank you.'

Andy and Des are the same two who were on the newspaper page that Duke showed me weeks ago. They stay around talking to me, to the other people there, or on their cellphones. In fact, everyone is on their cellphones all the time. I hear the blonde lady say to them both, 'You've gotta get out of here, boys. This is career-ending.'

Andy's voice rises to a squeak. 'Career-ending? Is that all you're bothered about, Celia? Two kids have gone missin' and another one has appeared from nowhere with a monkey! I'm not budgin' till I know they're safe, career or no career.'

Des nods his agreement and mutters, 'Well said, mate.'

They both sit down on the big blue sofa and fold their arms defiantly. Celia slinks off, stabbing her cellphone with her finger.

We have been here in the room – people are calling it a 'studio' – for a while now, and there are still lots of people around. As well as Melissa and Freddie, who are nice, there are two or three policers, someone called a 'family liaison officer', who also has a uniform on, the lady called Celia who says she is 'Andy and Des's producer', but I do not know what that means, a man who says he is the 'manager of Tyne View Studios', and I do not know what *that* means, either. Andy and Des are still on the sofa, not saying much, but – along with Melissa and Freddie – their presentness is a little bit comforty.

Everybody else is talking all the time.

All the time. To me, to each other, or to their cellphones, and – despite Melissa's warning – 'taking pictures' of me and Pierre with the same devices, and the pictures appear immediately on the back of them and then disappear.

I suppose my wish has come true in one way at least. I am alive in the Wonder Age.

But now all I want to do is go back home.

CHAPTER 27

We have come out of the big building to face a crowd of people and yet more flashing cameras and shouts of, 'Over here, love!' and, 'Hey, future girl! Monkey! Look this way!' and when I do there is another storm of flashing.

Andy and Des stayed back in the studio. 'If we go out with you, the chaos'll be worse,' said Andy while Des nodded a lot.

'Good luck, Ocean,' he said.

'We've done a few telly pranks in our time,' said Des. 'And, if that's what this is, then it's the best one in history. Well done.'

'But it is not,' I said, and they both smiled. I think they understood that this is no prank.

On one side of me, the policer has her arm round me; Melissa does the same on the other side, while both my arms are clutching poor Pierre, who is trembling with scaredness. Freddie follows close behind with the Time Tablet now wrapped in a cloth bag.

'Ignore them, Ocean,' says the policer. 'They mean you no harm; they're just interested. See that people carrier there? That's where we're going.' Then she turns to the assembled crowd. 'We will keep you informed of any developments. I remind you that this is still a potential crime investigation, although it seems to me that we're sailing in uncharted waters – yes, Matt, you can quote me on that. If you wish to stay on the right side of the law, remember that minors are involved. I don't expect to be making any further comments this evening.'

Inside the big motorcar, the door slides shut with a swish and the car starts to move. Melissa breathes out shakily and lets out a long wail of heartache.

'My boy! Where is he? Oh God, Freddie, tell me he'll be all right?'

Freddie squeezes her hand and says, 'Hey, hey . . . it's okay. We'll get him back. We'll get him back. Won't we, Ocean?'

I nod my head with as much sureness as I can because this poor lady is so sad, and she has been very nice to me. I look through the glass to see so many cars! They are everywhere I look. With every new thing I see, another twenty questions pop into my head.

The lights, for example. Everywhere there are lights of every colour imaginable. All the cars have lights. On some streets, it is almost like daytime. Do people need that much light in 2023?

We have stopped next to a red light on a tall pole,

and the driver is looking up at it. Some young women, none of them wearing many clothes, cross the road in front of us, walking wobbly in high shoes. They all carry cellphones, and one stops in front of our vehicle, peering through the front glass.

'Ee! Look! Shellie! Linzie! It's them! I seen it on Twittah! That Andy an' Des thingy!' She raises the black rectangle to face us as the light on the pole turns to green. Ahead of us, another light starts flashing blue, followed by a loud wailing sound, and suddenly we are driving faster as the group of women and other cars get out of our way.

We pass groups of people standing outside taverns with drinks in glasses. They turn to watch us as we pass, and one group of men cheer and say, 'Wha-hey!' Then there is a whole row of brightly lit shops, all with colourful displays outside of fruit and vegetables of every kind. The houses and buildings are 'credibly clean, with glass in all the windows, and roofs that are in one piece.

Then we go past some metal gates and some more uniformed officers, these ones holding big black guns across their chests, and I see a sign saying NORTHUMBRIA POLICE.

A policer meets us as we get out of the car, carrying a large box with a caged front. He smiles and gestures to Pierre. I clutch Pierre tighter and shake my head. 'It's regulations, pet,' he says. 'We cannit have monkeys roamin' round a police station.'

'But he is not "roaming round", is he? Besides, I do not think there is room in there for him.'

'Oh aye, he'll fit all right. Might have to cram him in a bit, but . . .' He opens the caged front and reaches out to take Pierre, who bares his teeth.

'No! He is *not* going in there!'

'Listen to me, love. This is a health-and-safety requirem—'

The policer who travelled with us, who I now know is called Hannah – 'just Hannah, pet, we don't need to bother with titles' – steps between us and says to the man, 'We allow guide dogs in this police station, don't we, PC, erm . . .' She looks at the badge on his chest. 'PC Grainger?'

'Erm . . . aye, of course we do, ma'am.'

'Well then – this is a guide monkey, all right, constable?'

'But . . .'

'No buts, constable. Kindly step aside.' She waves her hand, and we all troop past. Pierre sticks his tongue out as we pass and, even though I know it is a coincidence, the look on the young policer's face is priceless.

Inside, countless pairs of eyes watch us as we are bundled through corridors until we arrive at something labelled FAMILY INTERVIEW ROOM with a fuzzy blue carpet and low green sofas. A black television is attached to the wall, but it is not switched on, and I am 'cited to see a food-selling machine in the corner a bit like the one Monsieur Lumière had. Pierre makes straight for a bowl of fruit and picks up a banana. I do not know if he has ever had a banana before – I certainly have not. He sniffs it, then he takes a big bite from the middle and starts chewing. Poor Pierre: he is probably quite hungry.

Hannah says, 'Are you hungry, Ocean? Help yourself. We'll get you some pizza; how's that?'

I have no idea what a pizza is, but it sounds like food so I say, 'Yes, please,' and then I take a banana. I bite into it the same way that Pierre did and start to munch. The outer bit is rather tough, but the inside is soft and sweet. I look up to see everyone staring at me, 'stonished.

'I think I'll have one as well,' says Freddie. Taking his banana in one hand, he breaks the black end and then peels off the yellow skin in three pieces before taking a bite.

So that is how it is done! I love that Freddie did not say anything to shame me, but he gives me a wink when he sees me copy him. Bananas go straight to the top of my list of delicious things to eat, even ahead of Nanny Moo's fish biscuits.

And so begins hour after hour after hour of telling my story, of being questioned by people in uniform, by others who are not in uniform. It is all a blur. They ask me 'gain and 'gain what my full name is and where I live, and my next of kin, and my birthday. I am taken to a side room and examined by a doctor. She weighs me by making me stand on a thing with a little screen with numbers that change, and tells me I have head lice (I already know that) and takes a 'DNA sample' (I do not know what one of those is) from inside my cheek.

Two huge, round bready things with tomato and cheese on arrive from somewhere in flat cardboard boxes. These are pizzas, and they now beat bananas into second place for delicious things. Pierre has already eaten another banana and now has two triangular pieces of pizza with its weird stringy cheese, which he gets all over his face and spends ten minutes picking out of his fur. I realise that I have not seen a single skinny person; perhaps all this lovely food is why.

They ask me about the Time Tablet and how it works. I say I do not know. One man wants to take it away 'to forensics', but Freddie and Melissa say no.

'It may be her only chance of getting back,' says Melissa.

The man is pushing the 'on' button repeatedly. 'I'm sorry, madam, but . . .'

Melissa stands up and snatches it back from him. 'Are we under arrest?' she says.

'Well, no, madam, but . . .'

'In that case, you may *not* take this without a warrant, and you'll need a magistrate for that, so, with all due respect, I'll be looking after it!' She gives the man a stern look. 'I'm a legal clerk, in case you were wondering. I know this stuff.'

Hannah the policer says to me, 'Now, Ocean, is there anything you want to ask us?'

I have been here about four hours, and I have already had quite enough of the Wonder Age.

'Yes,' I say. 'Can you get me home? That is, home to 2425?'

The silence that follows makes me feel cold.

CHAPTER 28

It is very late when we get back in the car. My mind is still racing, but I find my eyelids drooping. Only every time they do, I get an image of a broken-toothed man with boils, and hear his heartless cackle, so I force myself awake.

The police people wanted me to stay at the station, and Melissa had to be very firm.

'She's coming home with us,' she said. 'It's way past midnight. She needs a shower and a bed. You can station someone outside our house, and we'll resume in the morning. Do not come before nine.'

Soon we are on a much wider road and going so fast that I am terrified and clutching Melissa's hand tightly on one side, and Pierre's on the other.

She says to the driver, 'Can you slow down a bit, please? We have a nervous passenger here.'

'Have you been in a car before?' says Freddie.

'Not one that could move. Unless you include Monsieur Lumière's Wonderbuggy.' I see his brow crinkle in confusion, but I cannot explain everything to him straight away and, besides, as we come over the brow of a hill, I gasp at what I see.

On either side of the wide road are row after row of neat houses, all illuminated by lines of lights on top of poles. The trees are evenly spaced, and the hedges trimmed level. Small patches of grass form tiny gardens with bushes and flowers, with yet more motorcars parked on the streets. Even though it is late, lots of the windows have lights in them.

'Is . . . is this the coast road?' I say, and Melissa nods.

'Do you know it?' she says.

'It is not like this. It is broken and cracked and flooded. And there are . . . boars. You know – dangerous pigs.'

Soon there are fewer cars (our driver calls it 'the traffic'), and I can see the sea glinting in the cloudy moonlight ahead of me. We turn left along the seafront road – my road to morning school – and past the broken church, which is not broken now, with all its windows and walls intact.

'Stop!' I say. 'Stop right here! This . . . this is where it all happened.'

I get out with Pierre, and the others follow. It is night-time and the church is locked up; Freddie pushes on the huge wooden door, but it does not budge. The police car is parked on the road, its engine running.

Behind us, a man clears his throat and says, 'May I

help you? I'm the vicar of this church.' He looks at the watch on his wrist. 'It is a little late.'

Inside the church, the vicar turns on the electric lights with a number of switches by the door and I stand, transfixed, at the sight of the building in which I stood only a few hours ago when it was a ruin. The roof is complete; every wooden bench is in place and polished with little cushions dangling on hooks on the back; a sweet, smoky smell hangs in the air.

'Is this . . . the monkey? The one that fell from the future?' asks the vicar gently. He reaches out to scratch Pierre's scalp. He is quite old, with the kindest eyes.

I stare at him, stonished. 'How do you know?'

He waggles a cellphone in his hand and smiles. 'News travels fast. People are saying the most extraordinary things. May I ask why you wanted to come in here?'

'This is . . . where it started. Right there, in fact.' I point to the spot in front of the pulpit where Monsieur Lumière had stood, where the crossbow bolt had zipped over my head.

'And you say you've come here from . . . the future?'

Melissa steps forward and murmurs, 'She's very tired, Reverend. I don't think she wants to answer any more questions.'

'It is all right. I do not mind,' I say. I quite like this 'reverend' man. He has a friendly face. Sort of young, but old at the same time. I turn to him and say, 'Yes. I live not far from here in the year 2425.'

'And the church still stands? How very reassuring!' He closes his eyes and nods slowly and contentedly.

I do not have the heart to tell him the truth: that although it still stands it is a crumbling ruin. Instead, I say, 'I am glad you do not disbelieve me. A lot of people do.'

He opens his eyes and looks intently at me. 'The world is a mystery, Ocean. Its purpose is a mystery too. Sometimes all we can do is have faith. And faith is perhaps the greatest mystery of all.'

I do not really understand this, but it sounds nice, and he is being kind, so I smile. 'Can we go now?' I say to Melissa. I take another look at the church, marvelling at how much beauty can be created from dull grey stones.

'Here we are: Tiverton Close,' announces the driver.

We have stopped outside a small, neat house on a street not far from the seafront. Looking out of the window, I recognise the house. It is just that the last time I saw it, I was with Duke, and it was covered with ivy and Duke was kicking the door in.

The blue flashing light on top of the car had stopped a while ago, but still there are people coming out of the nearby houses to look at what is happening. Once again, they all have their cellphones held up in front of them, some of which have tiny bright lights on the front.

'No secrets these days,' says the driver, turning round in his seat. He winks at me and chuckles. 'They've all been following it on Twitter and the socials. Do you know how to dance, pet? You could be a TikTok star, eh? Specially with that monkey!'

I smile, but I do not understand a word of what he just said, specially about being a 'tick tock star'.

As we get near the house, a man pushes forward. 'Hey, Ocean – can I get a selfie?'

I look at Melissa because I don't know what he means, and she tells him angrily, 'Push off!' She whispers to me. 'He lives two doors down. Don't know his name. What a cheek!'

Inside the house is so warm that I am falling asleep almost as soon as I walk through the door, but I keep wanting to look at everything. There are lights everywhere, and it is all clean and smells nice. Pierre and I use the toilet, and I flush it by pushing a button. Melissa helps me undress, and I stand under a hot, hot shower for the first time in my life, and I use lots and lots of soap (which smells of strawberries) from a plastic bottle. Melissa gets me to put it on my hair as well (another first) and then, wrapped up in a huge, fluffy towel that smells of flowers, I sit in front of her on the toilet with the lid down, and she combs my hair 'gain and 'gain until there are no lice left. Next I open my mouth while Melissa cleans my teeth with a vibrating stick with mint-flavoured stuff on it.

While she is doing this, there is a buzzing sound in her pocket, and she pulls out her cellphone. On the front is a picture of a lady and beneath it the word 'Sis'. Melissa sighs, switches off the mouth-stick and touches the device.

'Hi, Ailsa . . . yep, she's here . . . She's so tired . . . No, they're both still, well, wherever they went to – 2425 if you believe that . . . I don't think we have a choice but to believe it. Nothing else fits . . . No, the police have turned the place upside down looking for tricks or illusions, you know? Seems like your Kylie is an even bigger genius than you thought . . . No, I'm not *blaming* her, Ailsa, it's just . . . Yes, I know you're upset . . . we're all upset . . . Oh, don't be like that . . . Ailsa? Ailsa?'

Melissa breathes the deepest, saddest sigh I have ever heard in my life. The cellphone drops from her hand, and we end up in another embrace, my nose buried in her hair (which smells of trees, by the way).

When we separate, she holds my shoulders and says, 'Ocean? I bet your Nanny Moo wants you back home as much as me and Freddie want Thomas back, and my sister wants Kylie back. If wishing for something hard enough could make it happen, then we wouldn't have to worry, would we? But it's not. All we can do is have faith, yeah? Like the vicar said. Okay?'

I nod. 'Yes. I mean, yeah.'

'Pinkie promise?' she says, holding up her crooked little finger. I do the same and our fingers entwine while she gives me a sad smile.

I can hear Freddie's booming voice downstairs. He, too, is on the phone.

'From where? Is there no one nearer? Well, bring him back from holiday then! All right, I'll speak to him on his yacht.'

I am in Kylie's soft, comfortable bed. Melissa has picked up lots of clothes and shoved them in a tiny cupboard so that at least the small amount of floor space is clear. A long U-shaped desk with three computer screens goes round the room, and the shelves are crammed with cables and plastic things with wires and pieces of . . . well, I do not know what it all is.

Melissa sits on the bed and strokes my head as I snuggle down in the pillows that smell of cucumber. I can feel the reassuring weight of Pierre by my feet: he is fast asleep, although he is breaking wind silently and 'stremely whiffily. He is not used to bananas or pizza.

Freddie puts his head round the door. He wrinkles his nose.

'Is that a normal smell for a monkey?' he says. 'Phew.'

He is holding the Time Tablet, and he puts it down on the desk.

'Just spoken to some fella who turns out to be the

senior computer analyst for MI6.' He turns to me. 'That's a government intelligence agency.'

(I am not even sure I know what one of *those* is, either, but it sounds important, and that is probly a good thing.)

'Trouble is, he's sailing in the Caribbean at the moment. Won't be back till next week. Anyway, he's agreed to look at Kylie's computer when he gets to Miami in two days' time. There's a woman from the university who can patch Kylie's hard drive to a cloud server to enable remote access . . .'

'Wait, Freddie, wait,' says Melissa. 'Say that again in English.'

Freddie tries, and Melissa nods, but all I understand is that nothing will happen until somebody from 'Em-eye-six' goes to Miami next week. Perhaps the weather has to be overcast because Freddie keeps mentioning 'clouds'.

Anyway, next week is too late.

'It needs to be tomorrow,' I say, suddenly wide awake.

'Why is that, pet?' says Freddie.

'Because . . . because Kylie said so. There's another chance to make the Time Tablet work, I think,' I say. It sounds lame because it is. I cannot even remember what Kylie said. It was written on the back of the photograph with everything else in the box that Duke and I dug up.

Two chances on two consecutive nights. I remember that. We have already used up one of them.

'Where do you think Kylie and Thomas are now?' says Freddie, quietly.

I shake my head. 'I do not think it is a question of where, but *when*,' I say.

CHAPTER 29

THOMAS

The fallen tree that blocks our path is now only metres away.

'Oh my hat! *Stop!*' Duke yells as the Wonderbuggy's engine roars even louder, and the tall exhaust pipe pumps out more choking fishy smoke. I look over the side of the vehicle, ready to jump off before we crash.

'Hang on to your holly-ollyhocks!' shouts Monsieur Lumière from the driver's seat, and a second later the vehicle swerves violently to the right. I almost lose my grip, while from inside the cabin there comes a loud crashing and a tinkling as the contents are thrown around as if in a tumble dryer.

With a scream of the rattling engine and more choking exhaust fumes, the Wonderbuggy's massive tyres dig into the steep bank where there's a gap in the thorny hedges just wide enough to let us through. But the engine is not powerful enough and halfway up the vehicle stops, its tyres spinning in the thickening mud.

'Off! Off! Everybody off and push!' cries Monsieur Lumière. 'It is our only 'ope!'

He has to be joking? Behind us, our pursuers have abandoned their horses and are coming after us on foot, tempted by the prospect of fifty crowns for handing Pinker the Time Tablet. When I see the man who was thrown from his horse reloading his shotgun, that decides it.

'Come on, Kylie!' I shout. Duke is already at the back, shoving his skinny shoulder into the rear of the Wonderbuggy.

Perhaps it's because the vehicle is now lighter without us hanging on to it – whatever – but, with a further roar from the engine, the wheels bite into the mud and propel the tractor up the bank as, led by Pinker, the first of the people chasing us start to scramble through the gap we've left.

'Go, go, go!' shouts Duke, pausing only to grab a rock and make a well-aimed throw at Pinker, which connects with his skull, causing him to yell in pain. For a skinny kid, he's a very good shot.

Leaping back on, this time I hook my arm round a metal bar running the length of the tractor's roof. Kylie is now inside the cabin, Duke's hanging on to the other side, while Monsieur Lumière stands above the steering wheel, which is wobbling alarmingly, dodging the low branches that hang over the path we've found ourselves on. Then he sits down heavily, pulling a strap across his waist and buckling himself in as the tractor bounces violently.

I take a deep breath and look back. The people chasing us are further behind now, which is a relief. But then I notice that stretching far into the distance are two thin parallel lines of shining steel.

We're on a railway line. I look down and see that the Wonderbuggy's fat tractor tyres are widely spaced and sit either side of the tracks, bumping over the wooden sleepers that connect the rails.

Do they have trains here? Surely not. They don't even seem to have cars. But then why are the rails so shiny? Surely that means they're in use? And, if they are, that means that there's a chance we'll meet a train on them . . .

There's a loud clank, and a long metal tube bounces from beneath the Wonderbuggy and on to the tracks.

'Exhaust!' shouts Monsieur Lumière. 'It was loose anyway. We need to get this thing off these rails!'

You don't say, I think. Trees, bushes and branches are growing very close to the tracks. A low branch whacks the chimney and sends it flying on to the track behind us. It seems as though the entire Wonderbuggy is disintegrating under us. Kylie clambers out of the space in the door, coughing at the foul fishy engine fumes that are swallowing us up.

All three of us are now clinging to the top of the tractor cabin, trying to avoid being decapitated by low branches, when the worst thing that could happen . . . actually happens.

'Train ahead!' shouts Monsieur Lumière as we round a bend, and, sure enough, heading straight towards us – very fast – is a single-carriage passenger train being pulled by an ancient smoking engine.

With all his strength, Monsieur Lumière yanks the steering wheel violently to the left, and the tractor begins to turn before there's a dull crack and the wheel breaks off in his hands. Ahead, the train lets out a whistle of warning, and its wheels scream and throw off sparks as the driver applies the brakes, but the two vehicles are certainly going to collide.

'*Jump!*' shouts Monsieur Lumière.

Duke leaps off first, and I see him roll down the embankment into a huge patch of thorns. Kylie is next, off the other side.

What is Monsieur Lumière doing?

I'm closest to him, and I can see him pulling at his seat belt, unable to unbuckle it – seemingly the only part of this disintegrating vehicle that won't break away. His actions become ever more frantic as the train gets ever closer. The next two seconds seem to last forever. He stares ahead, eyes popping, his hand desperately scrabbling at the buckle. He glances at me, his face full of fear and sadness.

'Go, my boy – go now and bring back Ocean! It is

too late for me!' he shouts. 'Just go! *Adieu, mon ami!*'

With his free arm, he pushes me away from the Wonderbuggy, and I fall backwards, hitting the ground hard. Seconds later, the train and the Wonderbuggy collide in a crunch of metal and smoke and shrieking brakes.

Dazed and wincing from a sharp pain in my ankle, I scramble on to my hands and knees, and look up. The train, its brakes still screeching, has continued its journey down the track, pushing the mangled Wonderbuggy before it and back round the bend we'd come from. It's out of sight for a few seconds, and then there's a dull, low boom, and a cloud of smoke and flames appears above the trees, followed by the sound of falling pieces of metal. I imagined that one of them was the Time Tablet, now incinerated along with any hope of getting back to 2023.

I don't know how long I stay there, the rain lashing down now, soaking my best clothes and new trainers. I can't see out of my left eye, and, when I put my hand to it, it comes away sticky with blood. The sounds of the explosion, and Monsieur Lumière's last words, 'Goodbye, my friend,' seem to be stuck on replay in my mind. I cover my ears in a vain attempt to stop the noise, and lower my head.

And then, days later – or more like minutes really – I hear, 'Tommo? Tommo? You all right, mate?'

CHAPTER 30

'The . . . the Time Tablet?' I croak. It's the first thing I think of.

Kylie slumps down in the mud next to me. Her wild hair is plastered to her skull by the rain, and her glasses have been bent out of shape. She shakes her head.

'You saw what happened, yeah? To the tractor-thingy we were in?'

She nods. 'Yeah, I saw that. Poor bloke? He tried to save us.'

'And what about the kid with the hat? He jumped, didn't he? Did you see him land?'

Kylie shakes her head again, and we sit in silence for a moment or two.

'What are we going to do? Do you . . . do you want to go back and check on them?'

'There's nothing we can do to help, mate. They've all gone. If that kid made it out, he'll have scarpered already. And, from the looks of them, I'm not keen to get any closer to that lot than we've already been. I mean, jiminy: one of them had a crossbow! *That's* how much he wanted the Time Tablet.' Kylie coughs and spits, then says, 'Do you know where we are?'

I point beyond the bushes. 'The sea's that way – I think. But it's not just where we are, Kylie. It's . . .' I tail off, almost unable to say this. 'It's *when*.'

We're both standing now, looking down the train track. The rain has settled into a steady drizzle; we couldn't be wetter anyway. 'Kylie, have we actually travelled in time?'

She puffs out her cheeks, then nods slowly. 'I think we have. But it was never meant to happen like this. Something must have . . . I dunno. Gone wrong. You know – with the Time Tablet?'

Gone wrong. That was my fault, wasn't it? I shiver all over with guilt, but it looks the same as shivering with cold so Kylie doesn't notice.

'It makes no difference now anyway,' she says. 'The Time Tablet's gone up in smoke, and we're gonna be worse off if we stay out in this rain.'

'Can . . . can you make another one?' I hardly dare ask.

She thinks about this for a bit. 'Depends, Tommo. Depends on the technology they have here, which, from the looks of it, may be a challenge? I mean – look at these houses. What the heck's happened here?'

I'm still half mad with shame for my part in wrecking the Time Tablet's programs. I guess it's this that makes me scramble to my feet, wincing in agony at my twisted ankle, and push through the bushes away from the railway tracks and towards the tumbledown houses.

I want to do something right at least. 'Shall we find out?' I say.

Soon we emerge on to what was once a street, with the remains of houses and buildings shrouded in dripping creepers and ivy. The rusting carcasses of cars, almost invisible beneath the greenery, line the cracked road. Kylie whistles in amazement.

'This is . . . this is . . .' she begins, but doesn't finish, just shaking her head in disbelief.

'Look!' I say, hardly able to believe my eyes. Right in front of us is a rectangular building, as ruined and decrepit and overgrown as the rest. Except I can make out three letters on the wall.

R R Y

A metal pole stands in front of the building with a vine twisting up it.

'Can't you see?' I say. 'It's the Quarry! The Quarry pub. Where we had lunch with Mam and Dad last Sunday. That pole there – it had the pub sign hanging from it.'

Kylie's jaw hangs open in astonishment. She wipes rain from her face and stares again, dumbstruck.

'Which means . . .' she drawls, thinking carefully, 'that along this road and to the left . . .'

I've already started limping down the road. 'Is Tiverton Close. Come on!'

I honestly don't know why I'm so excited by this. I guess, with everything that's happened in the last hour being so incredibly, unbelievably strange, I'm ready to grasp any little thing that's even vaguely familiar and hold it tight.

My twisted ankle is less painful now, but I still can't run on it, although the cut above my eye has stopped bleeding. Kylie catches me up, and in the purple twilight we head down the broken road carpeted with dead leaves. There are unfamiliar bird calls coming from the darkening trees; a fox barks, and a pair of bony stray dogs emerge from the undergrowth to look at us with flashing eyes, then they slink back into the shadows.

Suddenly there's a crashing noise in the bushes.

Kylie grabs my arm. 'What was *that*?' We both freeze.

And then it comes again. A loud rustling, and the movement of something – something big – in the undergrowth, this time accompanied by a deep, growling grunt.

'It's an animal,' I say.

Kylie hasn't taken her eyes off the spot where the disturbance came from. 'Well done, Einstein,' she murmurs. 'Unless it's someone with a crossbow? Let's just keep going, shall we?'

'We should sing,' I say, trying to keep the terror out of my voice as the grunting resumes.

'Are you mad, Tommo? Why should we . . .'

'I saw it on YouTube. You know: *Wild Survival*? Animals don't like noises. Singing scares them off. Come on, erm . . .' I'm trying to remember a song, any song. '*The wheels on the bus go round and round, round and round . . .*'

Kylie joins in. '*Round and round . . .*'

It makes me even more scared. I was expecting – hoping – for Kylie to say, 'Don't be a galah, Tommo. There's nothing to worry about.' But she doesn't. It's terrifying – definitely the most scared I've ever felt singing a nursery rhyme.

We're at the corner of Tiverton Close when whatever has been stalking us suddenly breaks cover from the bushes. A huge, hairy pig skitters to a halt and eyes us up.

'*The people on the bus go* . . . Oh jiminy, Tommo. That's one ugly pig.'

The massive boar is about twenty metres ahead of us on the road, the coarse hair standing up on its neck, and two broken yellow tusks poking up from its lower jaw. Steamy breath rises from it as it seems to consider its options.

'Any tips on avoiding an attack from a wild animal, Tommo? In the YouTube video?'

'Well, yes – but you're not gonna like it.'

'Try me. I mean, if it's an alternative to getting eaten by a wild pig, it's gotta be worth a try, eh, cuz?'

I take a deep breath and say, 'You've got to run towards it.'

'Oh crikey. *Towards* it? You don't mean that, do you?'

'Run straight at it. It'll run to meet you. And then, at the last minute, veer off at a forty-five-degree angle.'

'That's a bit precise, mate.'

'Just, just . . . veer off, all right? It won't be able to turn quick enough to get you. You go left, and I'll go right. Meet you at my house?'

'This works, does it – this running-at-a-diagonal-angle thing?'

The boar has started to gallop towards us, lowering its head for an attack.

'It had better!'

CHAPTER 31

The thing I hadn't said to Kylie was that the video I'd seen on YouTube had nothing to do with pigs, or boars, but was about bulls. They have these massive wild bulls in France that weigh, like, half a tonne, and young men in villages show off their bravery by running round them, millimetres from their sharp horns.

Will it work with a wild boar?

I'm about to find out.

The boar is picking up speed as it gets closer.

'Wait . . . wait . . . wait,' I say to Kylie. The boar lowers its head further. It's less than two metres away and will certainly charge straight into us, but then I shout, 'Now!'

Kylie goes left, and I go right, towards the pig, but diagonally, trying to ignore the agony in my ankle. It immediately turns its head towards me. As it passes, I swear I get a whiff of its earthy, piggy odour, but I'm way past it by the time it skitters to a halt. At this point in the videos I saw on YouTube, the bull would stop, and the boys would saunter over to the barrier where their buddies were waiting to high-five them. This wild pig, it seems, had not seen the video. Instead of stopping, bewildered at our brilliance, it starts to come at us again. This time, I am not hanging around.

'Keep running!' I yell, and we do, as fast as we can, towards what I can still just about recognise as my house. Like everywhere else, it's covered with greenery, and half the roof has fallen in, but it is – or was – definitely where I live. Lived.

There's no front door: just a space with a small mound of bricks where a chunk of wall has fallen off. I'm in the lead, with Kylie right behind me, and the vicious pig gaining ground with every step and grunting furiously. I leap over the bricks and a piece of broken door and hurtle through the doorway.

'Stairs!' I shout, and grab the bannister rail to haul myself up. With a splintering crunch, it comes away in my hand. Still, the stairs creak and complain, but seem to hold my weight. Kylie follows me, and we're halfway up when the boar scrambles over the bricks and squeezes through the front doorway, its sides scraping the doorframe.

It raises its head and looks at us with pure fury, panting and snorting. It's standing beneath the hall mirror, exactly where the doormat normally is, and it paws the ground as though wiping its feet.

Then it launches itself at us, thundering up the first few stairs and then stopping as Kylie and I retreat further.

We're on the little square landing where the stairs turn, and we can't go any further because the last few stairs aren't even there.

If I thought boars were that smart, I'd say this one had an evil grin. Its small black eyes are focused on us sharply, and it opens its mouth to show a red throat guarded by sentries of massive teeth. It seems to be climbing the remaining stairs deliberately slowly, one at a time.

I hug Kylie as we cower on our little square of landing.

Suddenly there's a cracking noise and a long splintering crunch as the entire stairway below us gives way under the weight of the massive pig. Wooden stairs, bannister rails and snorting beast cascade to the ground floor, leaving Kylie and me alone on the isolated landing. And then that gives way too, or at least the bit that's supporting me, and I find myself falling until Kylie's big hands grab my wrist, while my other hand desperately holds on to a broken wooden spar jutting out from the wall.

I'm only a metre or so from the ground. It would be easy to let go and drop. But then the dazed pig, covered with ancient plaster and debris, twitches, staggers to its feet and spies me hanging in front of it, like a strip of bacon dangling before a hungry dog.

'Don't drop me, don't drop me, Kylie, please!' I yell, and I feel her grip tighten on my wrist. The boar gives a terrifying grunt and snaps at my ankle. With a yelp, I snatch my foot out of the way, but the lace of my trainer is trailing, and I feel a tug as its jaws clamp down, and the pig starts to pull hard.

My hand holding the wooden spar loses its grip, and I can feel my other hand slipping out of Kylie's grasp as the beast tugs harder.

'I'm sorry, Tommo! You're going, mate!' wails Kylie, and a second later I crash painfully to the ground.

With a squeal that I swear is evil pleasure, the boar widens its jaws, and I see the ropes of saliva snap as it prepares to bite down on my ankle. Then, from behind me, comes a scream of, '*Yaaaah!*' and a dark figure appears from our front room, holding a massive axe above its head. In one action, the axe swings up and then down, into the skull of the boar.

Above me, Kylie murmurs, '*Ouch* . . .'

The boar staggers two paces, then its front legs buckle. With a throaty gurgle, the beast collapses, dead, its head on my stomach. It twitches once, twice and then is still. It's only then that I see who our rescuer is.

The bowler-hatted kid waggles the axe free from the head of the boar, then looks first at me and then up at Kylie, his single good eye shining in the twilight.

'You took yer time,' he says, then he looks out at what was the front path to my house. 'Is . . . is me uncle wiv ye?'

*

'This is the strangest thing, like . . . ever,' I say to Kylie.

We're in *my* house, where I've lived since I was little. Parts of it are the same: the sofa in the front room, for example, although it's now mouldy and rotten. I recognise a vase that Mam would put flowers in lying next to the dead pig. There are cobwebs everywhere. Mam would have a fit.

The three of us sit on the mouldy sofa anyway because it's a bit better than the floor. I've propped my still-sore ankle on the wonky coffee table that I remember Dad making. Next to it is a plastic bag. Poking out from it is the Time Tablet that the boy has rescued – not destroyed in the collision, after all. Neither of us dares to touch it. In fact, I can hardly bear to look at it, as though even my gaze might somehow damage our only hope of getting home.

Home? *I'm sitting in it.*

The boy, Duke, breaks the silence by saying, 'So . . . where are they? Ocean and Pierre? They were next to me and then . . . they weren't.'

'It wasn't meant to happen?' says Kylie. 'Not like this. But I guess, if Tommo and I are here, then she's . . . where we were? That is . . . the year 2023.'

We all let this idea settle in our confused heads.

Duke says, 'He is still alive, you know. My uncle. He'll think o' summink. He's very clever.'

'Sure he will, mate,' says Kylie, catching my eye. Then she does her awkward hugging thing on Duke, knocking

174

his hat off, and he doesn't mind. He even manages a weak smile, and I feel bad for ever thinking less of Kylie for being a bit weird. In fact, I'm beginning to think that Kylie's difference might be what makes her special.

We stay on the sofa for ages, firing questions at one another. For example, from Duke: *How does the Time Tablet work? What went wrong? What's it like to fly in an 'aerialplane'?*

From us: *What year is it?* And the big one: *Who's Pinker?*

Duke's reply stuns us.

'He's your *stepfather*?' says Kylie, her eyes wide behind her wonky glasses. Duke nods glumly.

'So what the heck does he want with the Time Tablet?' she says.

Duke says, 'He's a trader, a smuggler. Perhaps he wants to sell it? He'll do anyfin to get what he wants. And I mean anyfin.' He sighs and then looks at Kylie. 'He's a bit like you. Big brain. Knows a lot about computers, and how they work, y'know?'

Something here doesn't add up for me but I have too many other questions to let it hold me up. I say, 'Duke, can you explain again what happened? You know – to the world. Because, when we left it, it wasn't exactly perfect, but –' I gesture at the dead boar, still oozing blood on to the ground – 'we weren't attacked by wild pigs. We had houses, and cars, and mobile phones.'

'Yeah,' says Kylie. 'What the heck went wrong, Dukoe?'

CHAPTER 32

'What went wrong?' repeats Duke. He pushes back his battered black hat and scratches his shock of hair. 'I dunno, really. Apart from the meteorite. Most folk know that. We . . .'

'No,' says Kylie, holding up her hand. '*We* don't. What meteorite? When?'

Duke looks down at the ground, ashamed. 'I din't go to school, y'know. I mean, I'm not *heducated*, am I? I can read and reckon up in me head, and I can repair loads o' stuff, but I know nuffin' about *that* sort of stuff.' He waves his hand towards the Time Tablet. 'All I know is what everyone knows. That a meteorite hit the uff, and it bought a germ from outer space that spread on the wind in weeks . . .' Duke looks up and sees that Kylie and I are desperate to learn more, but horrified as well. He gets to his feet and starts pacing in front of the wall, right where we used to have our TV.

'Almost everybody was infected, but hardly anyone got sick. It just meant that no one could have babbies. It affected men and women the same. Infertility, they called it. With no babbies, there were soon no adults, and in two or free generations, everyfin just . . . stopped. That was the end o' the Wonder Age and the start o' the Great Silence. The whole world went quiet.'

'So . . . how come *you* are here? And everyone else?' says Kylie.

'Like I said, it infected *almost* everybody. Some folks, maybe one in a hundred, maybe less, they could still make babbies. Just not enough of 'em.'

When he says that, it makes us go quiet for a few moments. Then Kylie says, 'I can't believe the world has turned out like this,' unable to keep her voice from cracking with emotion. She looks at Duke. 'Sorry – no offence, mate? I mean, you're great and so on. But it's like we had *everything*, and it's all been taken away. All those great things that we can do. Could do, I mean. All that technology and – *poof!* – it's all gone with one little bit of space rock. It was little, wasn't it?'

Duke shrugs. 'Maybe a coupla metres across.'

'Couldn't it be, you know – deflected or something?'

He starts pacing again. 'That's what they said. They said that if they'd known, they could've *hanticipated* the coming disaster, and sent an aerialplane into space . . .'

I chip in here. 'Aeroplanes don't go into space, Duke. Rocket ships do, though.'

'A rocket ship, then, with a bomb or summink that would . . . oh, I dunno. Like in *Star Wars*?'

My jaw drops. 'You . . . you know *Star Wars*? Who's your fave—'

'When did this happen?' interrupts Kylie.

Duke smiles sadly. 'That's one fing everybody knows.

'In twenty hundred and forty-four,
The population grew no more . . .'

'In 2044. That's twenty-one years from now, Kylie,' I say. 'I mean, from then. Oh, I don't understand.'

We've been here about half an hour. All three of us are still soaked through and our teeth are chattering when I have an idea.

'Do you reckon we could get upstairs?' I say, looking through the doorway at the wrecked staircase.

CHAPTER 33

The aluminium stepladder is still in the place we kept it behind the kitchen door, 402 years ago. Using that, I climb back to the little landing, then I haul the ladder up and use it to span the gap to the top floor. Kylie and Duke follow and, once we're upstairs, we tread carefully, checking our weight with every footstep in case the old floor should give way.

'Look!' I say. 'This is my old room.'

I push the door and it falls inwards, sending up a cloud of dust. I step through, expecting, with a quivering stomach, to see my stuff. Maybe even my books and *Star Wars* duvet cover.

But it doesn't look like my room at all. The bed is here, covered in hundreds of years of dirt and mould; there's a computer screen on a desk, and books on the shelf. I pull one out and it's stuck to the others with mould. Ivy grows up the wall and covers most of the window, making the room even darker than it is anyway.

'That chest of drawers,' says Kylie. 'See? It's the one that was in my room. I recognise the handles.'

She's right. The wood is warped with age, and the drawers are hard to pull out. Inside, the clothes are rotting and unrecognisable. I pull away a thick cobweb, and a *massive* spider scuttles back into the darkness. In the very bottom drawer are packages in transparent plastic. I seize one excitedly.

'It . . . it's Mam's,' I say. 'Mam's favourite winter jumper!' My fingers are scrabbling at the plastic zip. 'Every spring, she puts our woollen stuff away so the moths don't get them.' I hold it up, and it seems so familiar. Mam's jumper: dark blue with a little white pattern on the cuffs and neck. I hold it to my nose for a few seconds, hoping it smells of her, but it doesn't.

'Here – there's one each for you. I think that one's Mam's as well. And Duke – this is Dad's Christmas jumper.'

I hand him a thick sweater that isn't in plastic, but hasn't rotted, probably because it's some man-made fibre. There's a picture of Santa Claus with a fluffy white beard hanging from the front and the words *Ho! Ho! Ho!* knitted into the pattern.

Dukes eyes it curiously. 'Who is that?' he says.

'Oh, mate, you don't have Santa Claus? Father Chrimbo? What sort of world is this?' Kylie looks at me, then says, 'Doesn't matter. At least it's dry and warm, yeah?'

The sweater reaches almost to Duke's knees. He lifts

it up like it's a dress and does a funny *rat-a-tat* dance with his feet. It makes us laugh so much that, by the time we're back downstairs, stepping over the dead boar in the hallway, we're feeling warmer and happier.

Then Kylie drops her Australian accent and says, in Geordie, 'Ee, Thomas, if I've asked you once, I've asked you a thousand times – don't leave your dead pig in the hallway for me to clear up!'

It's a perfect imitation of Mam. So perfect that, even though I try not to, I find myself starting to cry because I want to be with her so much that it hurts. Kylie comes up to me and, realising what she's done, says, 'I'm sorry, mate,' again and again.

Outside, the downpour has begun again with another thunderclap and rain being thrown at the window as though from a bucket. We're going to be here for a little while longer as the smell of the dead boar spreads through the house.

Still, we are not tired. We refresh ourselves with water from a broken drainpipe. Duke asks Kylie to tell him every detail of her flight from Australia.

'A double-decker aerialplane?' he says in disbelief. 'And they bring you food? Like in a restaurant? Wow! How long did it take? Did you watch a fillum?'

. . . and so on. Duke asks about *Star Wars*, and we both have to assure him that it's not a true story, which seems to disappoint him. In turn, we ask him about growing up in a world without television, or cars, or computers. He tells us about seeing whales swimming up the River Avon, and the huge clock face in London that rises above the water in the flooded capital. And more about Pinker.

'He ain't just some . . . bandit, y'know? Some gadgie on a horse wiv bad breath and boils. He's seriously, *seriously* brainy. Like you just would not understand.'

I glance at Kylie when he says this, but she's hanging on Duke's every word.

'Pinker was working on tryna build new computers when everyfin' flooded. Destroyed his work. He was always a bully, my uncle reckons, but that? It sent him crazy. Y'see: he saw the power of computers. If he could control them, build them, well . . . his power could be limitless.'

None of us says a word for the longest time, then my stomach gives a loud growl. The last thing I ate was a triangle of egg sandwich in the *Ministry of Mystery* green room.

Duke goes off to rummage in the dark kitchen, and I follow him. Our old fridge is still there. The rubber seal on the door has decayed and stuck, making it hard to open, but there's nothing inside anyway. In a cupboard above the sink, Duke finds some tins with labels that have rotted away. These ones are round and flat like a tin of tuna, with ring-pull openers. The contents smell fishy, but not rotten. I poke about with my finger. It's not tuna: it's something else familiar . . .

'Hand it over then, Tommo?' says Kylie from the doorway, and she digs into the contents. ''Scuse my fingers. I could eat a dingo's butt, I tell you.'

'Er, Kylie . . .' I say, but she's not listening.

She extracts a huge fingerful, which she pops in her mouth and chews for a second.

'Oof. Pretty highly flavoured, I'd say. What is it? Where's it from, Dukoe?' She takes another lump and offers the tin to me. 'Go on, Tommo – it's fine.'

Duke says, 'A lotta canned food survives, and if the tins ain't damaged it's usually all right. But most of it's unlabelled. Like this.'

Kylie pauses. 'Survived? You mean, from before all the bad stuff happened?' Duke nods. 'So this can is, like, four hundred years old? What the heck is it? It tastes ripper!'

I cough politely. 'Kylie. I think I know what it is.'

'Oh yeah?' She shovels in another lump.

'You know our cat, Korky . . . ?'

Kylie – being a genius – is not normally slow to catch on to things. But she continues chewing and says, 'Yeah. What about her?' I say nothing and let Kylie make the connections.

'Oh no,' she says at last. 'Oh jiminy. You're telling me

. . . oh heck, no!' She spits the contents of her mouth back into the tin. 'You're telling me I'm chowing down on four-hundred-year-old *cat food*?'

Duke starts to laugh as Kylie spits and splutters, and I join in.

'It's not flippin' funny, guys!' she croaks, gargling with rainwater, and that just makes us laugh even more. 'I could have been poisoned. It's a wonder the cats aren't all dead!'

She spits one last time, as our laughter's dying down, then she begins to giggle herself. And that just sets us all off again and, for the second time in an hour, that damp, dark and mouldy old house is filled with the sound of us laughing. I think Duke is crying with laughter, then he wipes his eyes and says, 'Wait till I tell Ocean . . .'

Finally, a cat appears at the door to the hallway, then another and another: bony strays attracted by the cat-food smell, or maybe the dead pig. One of them starts to lap at the pool of blood in the hallway. We open the remaining tins and share the food among them.

None of us says much as we watch the cats eat. I try to stroke one of them, but it hisses at me and I back off. After a while I look round and Kylie is not there.

'Kylie?' I call, then more desperately. 'Kylie!'

Her voice comes from the front room. 'Relax, y'great galah. I've thought of something.'

CHAPTER 34

Kylie holds a piece of wood from the broken staircase and her eyes settle on the boar's blood that is pooling in the doorway to the front room. She dips the end of the stick in the blood, then uses it to draw a large circle on our living-room wall.

'Okay, this is the earth,' she says, then she adds a dot outside the circle. 'And this,' she says, 'is Permasat. Solar-powered, launched quietly from the Kennedy Space Centre in 2022, designed to last hundreds of years . . .' She trails off, a little dreamily. 'Well, anyway, the satellite is still going. It has to be, otherwise how did we get here?'

In simple terms, as the earth rotates, Permasat stays put.' She taps the bloody diagram with her stick. 'That means we have to wait for the earth to rotate to bring the Time Tablet within Permasat's communication range. You with me?'

Slowly, like he's working it out, Duke says, 'So – we can activate the Time Tablet again in twenty-four hours?'

'In theory. Everything works in theory, Dukoe. A theory is like a plan of battle. And no battle plan ever survives first contact with the enemy – the enemy in this case being the real world.'

'That doesn't sound very hopeful, Kylie,' I say.

'Don't worry, Tommo. The second bit of the quote says, "What matters is how quickly the leader is able to adapt." So I think I'm the leader here, and we are going to adapt.' She sits down heavily on the sofa, making Duke and I bounce up. 'Only . . . I'm not sure how yet. We have one more chance in less than twenty-four hours. *If* I can get it to work.'

Again we sit in silence, this time for even longer, and I imagine I can hear the cogs in Kylie's megabrain grinding out an answer to our predicament.

If only.

Then she's on her feet again. 'The signal that's relayed to the satellite and back to earth,' says Kylie, pointing with her stick, 'is pretty weak. It has a very small footprint – only about twenty kilometres across at its strongest. But it can be made stronger with a combination of iron and water. Have you heard of the Shaxon Effect?'

I shake my head, and Duke says, 'Kylie, I told you I din't go to school.'

Kylie doesn't seem bothered. 'It's only a theory. Anyway, under the right conditions, the combination of water and iron acts like a big magnet, concentrating the signal. I don't suppose the bridge is still here, but if we can get to a big ship, say, that might work?'

I look across at Duke. He should know about ships. 'We have ships,' he says with a nod. 'There's one in Dover – it's huge. People live on it. It's called the *Queen Mary Two*. It ain't seaworthy, though. It's just in the dock, has been forever. And there's one in Scotland, on the Clyde. And . . .'

'No, mate. We need one now.' She sounds agitated. 'Come on, come on: What's nearby?'

Duke turns his mouth down in thought and shakes his head. 'We only have fishing vessels. Mainly sail. Pretty small.'

Kylie clicks her tongue in frustration. 'No good, no good. We need something massive. I mean tonnes.'

'The Tyne Bridge,' I say, remembering my school project, 'is seven thousand, one hundred and twelve metric tonnes. It's mostly steel, which is . . .'

'Ninety-nine per cent iron,' says Kylie, quickly. 'I know all that. *And* over a massive river! But, like I say, it's probably collapsed years ago along with everything else.' We look across expectantly at Duke who shrugs.

'Most of it's still there.'

Kylie gasps.

'Does this mean we can go home?' I say.

'Does it mean Ocean will come back?' asks Duke.

Kylie sounds genuinely baffled and runs a bloody hand through her tangled hair. 'I mean . . . I'm gonna have to do some repairs in there. The CPU, the silicon chip, the adapted processor . . . I'm amazed you don't have any of this stuff.'

Duke shakes his head. 'I said: all that has degraded. Computer memories, silicon chips and whatnot. I mean, there are no silicon chips left anywhere in the world. I told ye – it sent me stepfather mad . . .'

He pauses, as if he knows what he has just said. All of our eyes are drawn once again to the Time Tablet on the low table.

'There's at least one chip still left in the world,' I say, pointing at the tablet. We are silent till I say what all three of us must be thinking.

'No wonder Pinker's so keen to get his hands on it.'

'And if he does?' whispers Kylie.

Duke chews his bottom lip. 'It's . . . it's un . . . unthinkabubble. All that power in the hands of a fella who can beat a kid till he's half-blind . . .' He points to his dead eye. 'That was just for reading.'

None of us says anything for at least a minute as we ponder what we might be up against.

Then Kylie holds up a finger and says, 'Shh. Can you hear that?'

The rain has stopped, and the breeze carries the sound of a loud screech – like a referee's whistle. Then an amplified voice, through a megaphone.

'*Ooooo!*'

'What are they shouting?' I say. 'It sounds like . . .'

'*Duuuuke!*' It comes again. '*Duu-uuuke!*' Then another whistle.

'They're out searching,' says Duke, his mouth pulled tight in fear. My stomach twists when he adds, 'And you two as well, I'd say.'

CHAPTER 35

The voices and the whistling are getting closer. They're coming down the old railway line. If they have lights with them, it won't be difficult for them to see our tracks leading through the bushes and down the street.

'Footprints, mud, broken branches – they'll easily find us if they want,' says Duke. 'But hush . . .'

For a minute, the three of us sit in silence, trying to work out if they've gone past. When the next whistle sounds, it's obvious that they're coming closer, and will soon be here.

Kylie claps her hands. 'Right. I haven't gone through all this to be stopped by them,' she says through gritted teeth. 'Come on: we've got to get back upstairs.'

It's quicker this time because we know what to do, and we're scared. I go first, using the aluminium ladder like before and by the time Kylie's on her way up we can actually make out individual voices among the small crowd coming into Tiverton Close.

'More footprints here, Pinker!' shouts someone.

Kylie stops and hisses a swearword.

'Come on, Kylie, quick!' I say, but she's already climbing down. '*What are you doing?*'

She hops over the stinking dead pig and back into the living room when I hear another voice. 'Hurry up – they're gonna get away!'

A second later, Kylie reappears, holding the plastic bag containing the Time Tablet, which, in our haste, we'd left in full view on the coffee table. With one huge step, she's over the pig's corpse and scrambling up the ladder, and we can only hope that the metallic rattle of the aluminium steps can't be heard over the storm.

As Kylie hauls up the ladder behind her, the first of the searchers comes into the house. It's Pinker, breathing heavily and dripping wet. The three of us freeze on the landing, just out of sight of downstairs, trying not to breathe too noisily.

Pinker sees the dead boar, and he blows on his whistle furiously, summoning a crowd of about a dozen, all carrying fish-oil lamps. They gather in the hallway while I cower upstairs, shielded by the open toilet door.

'What the damnation is that?' says a man. He extends his foot and dips it into the pool of blood. 'Still sticky. This beast has been killed recently.'

'Oh, oh, oh,' moans a lady. 'What has become of young people today? The violence, the bloodshed, the . . .'

'Oh, be quiet!' says another man. 'This is Bikpik – the

hog that ate that kid's hand in Morpeth. Whoever killed this has done us a huge favour. It's only . . .'

He's interrupted by a scream from the front room. The same lady from the church rushes out. With a trembling finger, she points back into the room. 'Symbols! Eefil witchcraft symbols painted . . . *in blood*! Did I not tell you? And of Ocean Mooney no sign. She's been kidnapped, I tell you, by that strange travelling boy and the other two . . .'

Pinker holds his lamp up and looks around, making me shrink back behind the toilet door. 'Well, they ain't 'ere no more, are they? An' they can't be upstairs because there ain't no stairs.'

Another man approaches from the kitchen. 'Sign of some activity out the back, Mr Pinker. Digging or something. But looks as though it was done a while ago.'

I peep round the door again. There's a general tutting and shaking of heads, till Pinker says, 'That's it. They musta gone ahead of us. Let's keep looking. You – stay here in case they come back.'

The man he points to groans. 'Flamin' heck, Pinker. Stay here with a dead hairy pig?'

'You'll love it. It'll be just like a night in with your missus,' growls Pinker, ignoring the man's hurt expression. 'And the rest of you, don't forget – fifty . . . no, *five hundred* crowns for that Time Tablet.'

A few minutes later, and the whistles and shouts are

all but inaudible as the search party advances further into the distance. I hear the ancient sofa creak as our guard downstairs sinks on to it, and soon there comes the noise of heavy snoring. I feel like I can breathe for the first time.

CHAPTER 36

OCEAN

Lying, fearified, on Kylie's bed with Pierre at my feet, I do not sleep. Do these people really expect me to? I can hear crying coming from downstairs, and more conversations on cellphones.

This world, this so-called Wonder Age: it is not what I thought it would be. None of the tales I have read, none of the pictures I have seen, seem to say just how many people there are, how much noise there is, the lights, the cars, the cellphones, the shouting, the far-too-warm buildings, the exhausting activity. And I have only been here a few hours.

How do they do it?

The man asking for a . . . selfie, was it? And then Melissa had said something strange. She said, 'He lives two doors down. Don't know his name.'

How is *that* possible? Maybe there are so many people that there is not time to know the people nearest to you?

Pierre has crawled up the bed, and I hold on to his

little moist hand for a while before casting the thick covering aside and pressing the switch on the lamp next to the bed. Even that is amazing. One noise I cannot hear is oil-powered generators. I do not know where all the electricity comes from.

For once, everything is quiet and, for the first time, I cast my eyes round the room properly, trying to work out if there is any clue, any information that Kylie has left that will help me return to my time. Wearily, I get up and sit on the chair by the desk.

Every surface is covered with bits and pieces of stuff. Apart from ballpoint pens (I have seen them before, but never so many: she has a mug crammed full of them), there are books too (of course), and there are little plastic things with wires, bigger plastic things without wires, keyboards, a laptop computer with its keyboard removed, and three large computer screens all apparently linked together, with cables leading to a metal box with blinking lights beneath the desk.

Pierre picks up a toy mouse with little ears and a face drawn on to it. When he does, the centre screen of the three computers on the long desk glows light, with a white background and writing on it.

'Stop it, Pierre,' I hiss at him. 'Do not touch.' I take the mouse from him and replace it on the desk, and the printing on the screen moves. It is strange: if I push the mouse forward, the words move up the screen; if I pull the mouse back, they go down the screen. But, if I pick it up and wave it at the screen, nothing happens. I look underneath the toy: there is nothing but a tiny red light. It is not connected to the screen at all.

So I do it again, and move the words on the screen until they will not go any further. I start reading.

To: Kylie Woollagong
Cc: Melissa Reeve
From: Celia Taylor, BBC TV
Subject: Appearing on Andy & Des's *Ministry of Mystery*

Hi, Kylie and Thomas,

Just a quick email . . .

I gasp! So *this* is what an email is! Papa Springham had tried to 'splain once that it was a letter that got sent ''lectronically' between computers, but I did not, to be honest, really understand. And here is one, right in front of me, on a computer screen! I move the toy mouse a bit, and more words appear underneath.

. . . to say how much we are all looking forward to having you both as guests on our show on Saturday evening.

I have attached a timetable (below) that will give you details of the car collecting you from home, and the running order of the day.

As you know, this is a fun show, and your wonderful Time Tablet project will be the final item in the programme.

The interview that accompanies your appearance with your cousin, Thomas, will go like this. I have included your answers based on what you have told me already. Please do not feel you have to say these exact words: this is not a script!

1. 'Hello, tell us about the Time Tablet.'

Here you will tell Andy and Des what the Time Tablet is supposed to do, and how you will look into the future.

2. 'How is Thomas involved?'

Here you say why you came to the UK from Australia and how Thomas has become your best friend (possible comment from Thomas here).

3. 'How does the Time Tablet work?'

This is your chance to explain – not too technically, please! – about the solar megastorm creating a bend in space-time that will make the Permasat signal able to view the year 2425. This will be possible on two consecutive nights: Saturday 26 July and Sunday 27 July at 8 p.m. You mentioned that being close to iron and water is important, so you can point to the Tyne Bridge outside the studio window to show where this will be possible.

4. As we draw the item to a close, the boys will ask you to demonstrate the Time Tablet 'to see if it works'.

Whether it does (or not!), we will award you both with the Mystery Medal for your participation in the show.

Thank you both, and do not hesitate to ask any questions on the day.

With thanks and best wishes,

Celia R. Taylor

Producer Andy & Des's *Ministry of Mystery*

I read question 4 again. The writer of this email had said 'to see if it works'. It seems fairly clear to me that she was not 'specting it to. How shocked they must have been when I arrived with Pierre!

I sit there for a long time in the light of the desk lamp, making the words on the screen move with the mouse, but not daring to do anything else. And then I read it all one more time.

The third time I read it, I notice something else. Something that I had ignored before, but which now leaps out at me.

This will be possible on two consecutive nights: Saturday 26 July and Sunday 27 July at 8 p.m.

Iron and water . . .

The Tyne Bridge . . .

I read it again. And one more time to be sure. And then I shout so loud that Pierre squeals, breaks wind and scampers behind the drapes.

'Melissa! Freddie! Come and look at this!'

CHAPTER 37

THOMAS

With our guard fast asleep downstairs, Duke, Kylie and I curl up on the filthy beds and try to sleep.

As dawn breaks, I am woken, cold and shivery, by a noise downstairs and footsteps going up the front path and away from the house. I wait a while in case the man returns, and then I wake the others.

It's time to attempt some repairs.

In the bathroom, I wipe the tiled floor with my sleeve. Kylie removes the Time Tablet from the plastic bag and puts it down. She runs a blood-encrusted forefinger over the large crack that splits the black-mirror screen and tuts. Two wires have come loose, and the bit that's glued on to the back has melted slightly. Honestly, it's hard to imagine that this device was ever even supposed to work; now there appears to be no hope at all.

Kylie shakes her head. 'If only . . . I mean . . . if I knew *how* it had gone wrong, *why* it had gone wrong . . .'

'Are you able to fix it?' I say.

200

'Not for certain. Not without all my screens and backups at home . . .' She looks around, realises that this *is* home. 'Ah, you know what I mean. I can't even check, you know? The battery-saving program means I can't switch it on till tomorrow night. That is tonight, I mean. These wires need to be reattached, and I can't even do that without . . .' She slumps back on the toilet seat. 'It's hopeless.'

Then I have an idea. I leave Kylie and Duke in the bathroom and go out on to the landing, flinching as a big rat disappears into the shadows.

I've lived in this house since not long after I was born. I'm the only one with an idea of where Mam *might* have cleared stuff away to. The house has obviously been scavenged at least once, but not very well. The bedding has gone from the beds, for example, medicines and towels from the bathroom cabinets. But bulkier things – the beds themselves, for example – are all in place.

Let me tell you: there is nothing – nothing at all – quite as strange as walking around in my own house 402 years from when I left it.

Except my mind is racing so much that I'm having trouble working everything out.

The year was 2044, Duke said, when the meteorite hit the earth. But it didn't kill anyone. It just stopped people having children. I do a calculation: in 2044, I will be thirty-two years old. So I've probably left home.

That's why my room looks different. Yet Mam and Dad have kept some of my stuff on a shelf. I run my fingers across the hardback Harry Potters that had once been Mam's, leaving a trail through the dust. There's the swimming trophy I got in Year Five, now tarnished beyond recognition, and the Lego *Millennium Falcon* I got for Christmas when I was eight . . .

A framed photograph lies facedown on the chest of drawers, and I turn it over. There's a young man in a suit and a woman in a white dress, with a smudge of something sticky obscuring her face. I don't know them, I don't think, and I replace it.

One by one, I go through the cupboards, but they've all been scavenged for clothes, leaving only coat hangers. Mam and Dad's room is the same, but in a worse state because the window's broken and everything is damp and mouldy.

So Mam and Dad must have lived here after I moved out. Lived here, in fact, until they both . . .

I don't want to think about that.

'Found anything?' calls Kylie from the bathroom.

'Shush!' I call back.

'Why, mate?' she says, not unreasonably, I suppose. But it's hard to explain. It is, I guess, a bit like being interrupted while you're praying or meditating, but I can't really say that. So instead I say, 'Just . . . because.' It seems to work.

The spare room, where Kylie had been staying, still has the U-shaped desk in it, but all the computer hardware has been removed. In fact, the room is completely bare apart from a bedframe. There's evidence of rodents, probably rats to judge from the droppings on the desk.

'Spooky,' says Kylie from the doorway. 'Have you checked the cupboard?'

She pulls a door. It comes off in her hand and hits the floor, sending up a cloud of dust. She points to a plastic box on a top shelf, clearly labelled, in Mam's faded handwriting:

KYLIE'S STUFF

'Oh jiminy. Aunty Mel is quite the organiser, eh?'

We carry it and the Time Tablet back to my bedroom and pop open the clasps on the lid that has kept out over 400 years of damp.

Inside is a bunch of bits and pieces, and the only things I could name are a mini keyboard, some tiny screwdrivers and a soldering iron with an electrical plug on the end. Everything else is from the inside of a computer, and is as big a mystery to me as anything in the world.

Kylie murmurs to herself. 'SIM-card cloner, wires, more wires, ethernet, PCB, PCB . . .'

I interrupt. 'What's a PCB?'

She holds up a little green strip the size of a Juicy Fruit covered with silvery dots. 'Printed circuit board. If the memory disk is the computer's brain, then this little fella is the central nervous system. But these are all crocked. See here: mould. And here: that's just age degradation. Useless. Everything in here is useless.'

She grabs the box and tips the contents out on to my old bed. Then she picks up something in a little ziplock bag. It's like the other PCBs but orange.

'Unless . . .' she murmurs. She stares at the bag, turning it over and trying to see it better in the dawn light that's now beginning to squeeze through the gaps in the greenery outside the window.

'Unless what?' I hardly dare to ask.

'This was a prototype PCB for the Time Tablet. It's double-sided, with a copper coating on the top and bottom layers, and it's been pretty well preserved by the look of things . . .' She drifts off again, and I poke her thigh to bring her back.

'And? *And?*' I say urgently.

Kylie sighs and turns to me. 'Listen, mate. Any PCB, any computer memory with digital information, will degrade over time if exposed to air. Sometimes just a few years if it's not preserved properly. The plan was to seal up the Time Tablet properly so that it didn't degrade. And this fella too.' She shakes the ziplock bag. 'If I can replace the damaged PCB in the Time Tablet with this one, then we may have a chance. By the way, that's a pretty girl you've married.'

'What do you me—?' I follow her eyeline to the photograph I'd looked at on the chest of drawers. Kylie has wiped the photo clean of the smudge. I get up to peer closer, but when I reach out to pick it up Kylie leaps up from the bed and knocks the picture from my hands. It lands facedown with a tinkle of broken glass.

'No!' she shouts. 'I've just realised, Tommo. Think about it! This is already very, very weird. You don't want to know your future. It could . . . it could affect everything. What if you met this girl, and already knew you were going to marry her? Imagine that! Just . . . just leave it!'

Her tone is so know-all it drives me nuts. 'So, if that's the case, why did you invent the flippin' thing in the first place?' I shout back. 'Didn't you think?'

'It wasn't meant to be like this, Tommo! It was . . . it was an experiment. I didn't even know for sure that it would work. And then the whole telly thing happened, and I couldn't back down, could I? Besides,' she says with an accusing look, 'we wouldn't even be here if you hadn't done whatever it was you did!'

I feel cold all over.

'Me?' I say. 'H-how do you know it was me?'

'I'm not an idiot, Tommo. Brain the size of a planet, remember? I can tell when someone's acting all weird, but it was too late by then, wasn't it? Damage done. And all because of *you*. You couldn't stand big cousin Kylie coming into your cosy little life with Mummy and Daddy and Korky the blimmin' cat, could you? Because you want the whole world to be about you.'

Her face is right up close to mine now, and she prods me hard in the chest with each syllable. 'You. You. *You!*'

There are tears clouding my vision, and I push her hard so that she staggers back, grabbing the doorframe. She's about to come for me, I know it, and I cringe because in size and strength I'm no match for Kylie.

Just then, a voice shouts, 'Stop it!' and Duke leaps between us.

'What is wrong with you both?' he says.

Kylie and I point at each other.

'It's her!' I say.

'It's him!' says Kylie.

We stand there, pointing and panting, until we both realise that there's nowhere else for this to go. There's a long pause while we both breathe hard, eyeballing each other.

'There's only one fing we need to be concerned wiv, and that is – can you fix it?' says Duke to Kylie. 'Well?'

She puffs out her cheeks. 'I'd have a better chance if I knew what this . . . this total galah did to my program.'

And so there in the greenish dawn light I confess what I did.

'I pressed okay as some program was loading. There was a purple dialogue box on the screen asking something about a data transfer.'

She's waiting for me to go on. Only there is nothing else. 'That's it,' I say. 'I'm really sorry, Kylie. You're right. About everything. I was a total . . . galah.'

She nods slowly, but she's already thinking of something else.

'Bring the box? And the screwdrivers? I can't promise anything . . .'

CHAPTER 38

After half an hour crouched over the deconstructed Time Tablet on the bathroom floor, Kylie carefully pushes the cracked screen back on to the rear section, then she stands up to stretch her back and straighten her glasses. Her forehead is shiny with sweat, even though the day isn't warm yet. I've watched her progress in total silence; to be honest, I'm still feeling pretty rotten about our row.

She, though, seems to have forgotten it.

Duke has been quietly watching everything Kylie does and even pretends to understand her when she says things like, 'The principal program had an inbuilt override, which I disabled with a ping-pong muddle-flapper on the PCB frankfurter flange-switch . . .'

She didn't *actually* say that, I don't think, but that's what it sounded like to me. I'd drifted off to sleep in the bath for a bit, and I wake up when she says, 'That, my friends, is as good as it's gonna get.'

Duke and I exchange glances. For something that our lives depend on, it doesn't sound encouraging. The device now has even more wires coming from it, and the back panel seems loose. When I touch it, Kylie says, 'Careful: the glue may not hold.'

'Glue? Where did you find glue?'

Kylie points to an empty packet of Haribo Starmix sweets on the table. She'd stuffed her pockets from a large bowl of them in the TV studio green room.

'They're tasteful!' grins Duke. 'There was a ring, and a heart, and a fried egg . . .' He adds, a little sadly, 'Ocean would love 'em.'

The mention of Ocean hangs in the air like a fleck of dust. I don't think she's ever far from Duke's thoughts.

Kylie says, 'Yeah, well, we chewed them till we had a sticky paste? It's not perfect, but when it dries properly in the sun it should hold. Probably.'

'And is it going to work?' I ask.

There's a long pause. 'It might,' says Kylie at last. 'We need to get to the Tyne Bridge by eight tonight. The force is gonna be much weaker. If Ocean's in the same place or very near, that will help. There's a chance the thing will work again.'

This is new information, to me at least. 'You mean . . . that is . . . Ocean needs to be there as well? How will she know that?'

'I told the telly people that there were two chances for the signal to work. As we know, they just thought I was making the whole thing up anyway. But . . . someone may remember. There's a possibility Ocean may get to the bridge at the right time . . .' She tails off, surely realising that what she's said sounds, well, 'unpromising'? Then she mutters, almost to herself, 'Dammit.'

I glance over at Duke and then back at Kylie. 'Dammit what?'

'The instructions.'

'What instructions?' I say.

Kylie tugs her hair in frustration. 'They were on the back of a photograph stuck to the Time Tablet with Blu Tack?'

Duke nods, 'Aye, they were there when we unpacked it.'

Kylie's mouth is moving like she's trying to work it out before she says it. 'Well . . . in the studio those instructions were all still in my head. I was gonna type the instructions and put 'em in the box with the Time Tablet. Then, when we were in the church, Lumière picked up the Time Tablet and something fell off on to the floor . . .'

'I saw that too,' I say.

'I remember thinking how weird it was to see something that I hadn't even made yet. It kinda flipped me out, but then things got pretty hairy with horses and crossbows . . .'

Duke is ahead of me. 'So . . . now we might not be the only ones who know there's another chance of using the Time Tablet.'

Finally I have caught up. 'If Pinker knows . . .' I start, but Kylie interjects. 'Shut up, Tommo. We get it.'

One by one, we come down the aluminium ladder, Kylie carrying the Time Tablet, now wrapped in a blanket for safety. We're all a bit subdued. Already small clouds of flies are gathering round the dead pig, and I head outside to look at the hole by the yew tree. A huge bird that I don't recognise flaps overhead, cawing loudly. In the dawn, the wilderness surrounding us is coming to life.

Kylie comes up behind me. 'Weird, eh?'

'Which bit especially?'

She emits a tiny laugh. 'I'm thinking about the bit where we stand next to a tree that hasn't been planted yet, looking into a hole that we haven't even dug yet?'

'How does that even happen, Kylie?'

She says nothing. I think that means she doesn't know, so I try again. 'What about what that guy Pinker said? What was it? Something about if this goes any further, we're all doomed!'

'Yeah, I heard that.'

'And . . .?'

'I guess he meant that if we go back to our time and prevent the meteorite from striking, then this world here won't exist?' She turns and looks back at the decrepit houses.

'And . . .?' I repeat. 'Is he right?'

Kylie removes her glasses and polishes them on her woolly jumper. She replaces them and turns to me, head cocked, and takes a deep breath. *Oh boy*, I think, *here comes a long answer.*

'I dunno,' she says.

'You . . . you don't . . .?'

'Nope. Not for certain. I just think it's much more likely that we change *our* history and not this one. You know – we take a different fork in the road? We create a version of our future in which the meteorite doesn't strike earth. I mean . . . it's *Everywhen*. It's kind of consistent with Einstein's theories.'

'It is?'

'Sure. Though I don't think even ol' Albert would get his head round the fact that Duke and Ocean dug up the Time Tablet when I haven't even buried it yet.'

'Is it even possible to prevent a meteorite hitting the earth?'

She shrugs. 'Course it is. That is, if it's big enough. NASA have already tried it.' Then she looks back at the hole-that-hasn't-been-dug-yet.

'Okay. And what if it's not very big?'

'Practically impossible, I'd say. But I don't know.'

I feel like screaming. Kylie has a megabrain! How can she not know?

'Think, Kylie, think! This is important.'

'Crikey, Tommo, I didn't even know if it was possible

to make a Time Tablet. I just had an idea and ran with it. Sometimes that's just what you've gotta do? Trust your instincts, and if it doesn't come off then you start again.'

'Do you think it could be done then? Somehow?'

'You'd need to know which asteroid, I suppose, and how to find it in space, but yeah? In theory. A spaceship could alter the asteroid's direction simply by getting close to it, for example. A tiny gravitational shift would be enough. Or there's laser bees . . .'

'Don't you mean "laser beams"?'

'Nope. Bees. They're tiny-weeny spacecraft, only theoretical at the moment, but it's a heckuva theory. You see, the idea is—'

I cut her off. 'Listen, Kylie, even if we do get back home, the meteorite's still gonna strike us unless we create . . . what was it? A fork in the road – another future. So we need to know exactly which asteroid caused . . . all of this. So we can warn everyone.' As I wave my hand around, I turn to see that Duke has joined us. 'Duke – tell us the date it happened again?'

Duke says, 'The meteor strike? It was in 2044. Is that enough?'

I look at Kylie, who shakes her head.

'You'd need more info than that. Location of impact, speed, angle and so on . . .'

I'm on my feet. 'So how do we find this out? You all know this stuff, yeah?'

'No! We don't all know it. Do you know every detail of fings that happened centuries before you were born?'

'But you can find out? I mean, it's written down somewhere?'

'There's a lib'ry in Culvercot . . .' says Duke.

CHAPTER 39

The sun is fully up by the time we leave the house. The air is thick now, and steamy from last night's storm. Kylie has wrapped the Time Tablet in yet more padding, including a hand-made cushion cover that I remember used to be on our sofa. There's a mouldy old backpack in a cupboard and with that on her back she joins Duke and me as we head off up the garden path.

We're all scared that we might run into Pinker. Still, none of us says so. Duke has brought the axe, and when I asked him why he just shrugged and said it made him feel braver.

In daylight, the area that Duke calls 'the Bush' is slightly less creepy and forbidding than it was at night. We pass houses and shops that I can only just recognise through the dense foliage and sprinklings of tiny flowers. I yelp when there's a movement on the ground, imagining another wild boar. It's a squirrel.

Soon we're at the old railway line and, keeping out of sight, the three of us creep along to the scene of last night's crash. There's a crack beneath my feet, and when I look down I see I've stepped on an old record – a black disc like Dad's old vinyls, but thicker and more brittle. I hold it up, and when Duke sees it the corners of his mouth sag.

'"Rock Around the Clock",' he says. 'That was Ocean's favourite.'

Suddenly there it is, lying on its side halfway down the embankment: the blackened and burnt-out shell of the amazing vehicle we'd ridden on last night – the 'Wonderbuggy', half submerged in water. When I look behind me, Duke hasn't moved, his face frozen in horror.

'What if . . .' he stammers. 'What if he's . . . dead? And still here?'

He starts to look around, and his eyes fill with tears. I don't know what to say, mainly because I was wondering that myself.

Kylie paddles through the water to the Wonderbuggy's seat and picks up the seatbelt. 'Look at this, Dukoe: it snapped, but the buckle's still fastened. I reckon your uncle leapt free in time.'

Duke swallows hard. 'You sure?' The hope, the desperation in his voice is almost unbearable. Kylie's reply is firm and so convincing that even I believe her.

'Totally. With any luck, he laid low for a while and then made his way to hozzy.' She sees his puzzled look. 'Hospital? You have hospitals?'

Duke nods, but his eyes are cast down so he doesn't see Kylie glancing at me. We need Duke right now, and it seems kindest to allow him to believe his uncle's still alive. Besides, he might be. It's not a complete lie.

We walk the rest of the way to Culvercot in silence. By the time we get there through the forest of trees and crumbling houses and rusted cars, there's still hardly anybody about. I cast my eyes along the road, taking in the buildings overlooking the curved bay. 'It's almost recognisable,' I say to Kylie.

'If a bomb had hit,' she adds.

There's an old building at the end of the bay overlooking the sea called the Watch House, which is a community centre, but used to be a lookout spot for fishermen. It's still in pretty good condition. Kylie and I conceal ourselves behind its wall with a view of the library across the road. Duke hangs back. He's taken his hat off and turns it round in his hands while he stares out at the sea.

'What's up, Duke?' I say.

'I'm too recognisable,' says Duke with a worried expression. 'I mean – look at me.'

'So what?' says Kylie. 'Who's going to recognise you anyway?'

He joins us in peering round the wall. 'Do you 'member a craze old woman yesternight? The one shouting about witchcraft and Satan and everyfin?' He points at the building with a sign saying LIBRARY. 'She's the librarian. Frau Schwartz.'

Well, that changes things. I'd kind of thought that

we'd just saunter into the library and look up the information about the meteorite strike and, you know, job done. But we – or at any rate one of us – has to get past her first.

And Duke's right. Even without the Santa Claus sweater and bowler hat, he stands out, mainly because of his haystack hair.

'Sorry, Tommo, but I reckon I am too.'

Kylie's size means that she would also be recognised by anybody who'd been at the event last night. They both look at me. 'I went in the lib'ry once wiv Ocean. There's a history section at the back,' says Duke. 'Find the shelf labelled "Wonder Age". It's arranged by year. Look for 2044. Find the info you need, tear out the page and come back as quick as ye can. The old paloni will try and talk to ye – she tries to talk to everyone. Just say you're new here. Say you're from . . . Ireland or summink. It'll explain yer rummy accent.'

'My . . . accent? I don't have . . .'

'Shh. Chill out,' says Kylie. 'Now go. We've a lot to do today. If anything goes wrong, where do we meet? Duke?'

I don't like the sound of this. 'If anything goes . . .?'

But Duke isn't listening. 'You gotta go right now. Frau Schwartz has left the door open. We'll wait here. Bona fortune. Go.'

An old lady in long skirts that I recognise from last

night comes out of the library and shuffles two doors down to a shop with a hand-painted sign saying TEA ROOMS.

I take three deep breaths and walk as quickly as I can without trying to look obvious. It's only about fifty metres to the library, but it feels like five hundred. Without looking back, I slip inside.

The library is cool and musty-smelling. I go past the desk at the front. It's a small place – there are only four aisles of books, all arranged on rickety, poorly made bookshelves that look as though they could collapse at any minute under the weight they bear. I pick the aisle that isn't visible from the front desk and immediately go right to the end. There, as Duke had said, is a section labelled HISTORY.

Some of the titles I can see on the spines of the books, but most I can't so I start to pull out books at random.

The Reign of Queen Victoria

The Romans and the Britons

'Stay calm, Thomas. You've got plenty of time . . .' I tell myself even though I know I haven't.

The Tudors – the 118-Year Dynasty

The Rise and Fall of the USA

No, no, no! I emit a growl of frustration and push the last book back in forcefully. It dislodges another, which falls to the ground with a loud thump at exactly the moment that I hear the library door opening.

'Hello? Who's there?' comes an elderly lady's voice.

CHAPTER 40

To be honest, I didn't get a good look at her last night. I kind of had other things on my mind. Right now, she seems all right. Quite friendly, very 'librarian-ish'. She's wearing glasses and is holding a mug of tea in one hand and a bun in the other. She stands at the end of the aisle and eyes me with what might be suspicion, but could just be friendly curiosity. I am very nervous, after all.

She lifts up her cup. 'First time zere has been proper tea for months. You must have come in while I was out. Was there something special you were after, young man?'

Well, that's a good start. She doesn't recognise me.

'Erm . . . the, ah . . . the Wonder Age?' I stammer. Behind the librarian's head, I suddenly see exactly the title I need. In big red letters on a black background: *2044: The Year of Doom.*

She gives me a tight smile and sips her tea. 'And why would a boy like you be interested in such ancient goinks-on?'

She's just being friendly, Thomas, I tell myself. *Relax! Talk normally.*

'I, erm . . . er . . . school project.' Then I grin.

She hasn't moved nor has she taken her eyes off me. She speaks very slowly. 'That is nice. Which school do you go to, only your accent is . . . rather old-fashioned if you don't mind me sayink so?'

'I . . . I'm at, erm . . .'

Think, man, think! I see a book title in my eyeline. 'Saint Tudor's. It's in, erm . . . Dublin?'

'Really?' She smiles and swallows another sip of tea. I'm pretty certain she's swallowed my lie as well. 'You have come a long way. Stay right here. I have just the sing for you.'

She heads back to the front desk, and I'm alone in the aisle of books again. I grab the volume marked *2044: The Year of Doom* and start flicking through it frantically. I guess what I want is a single page headlined, THIS IS THE INFORMATION YOU NEED, THOMAS. Instead, it's page after page of small type, maps and charts.

Then I hear a key turning and the clunk of a lock, followed by a whirring sound. Edging to the end of the aisle, I see that the library door is now shut, and the librarian is at her desk, winding the handle on a wooden box while holding an old-fashioned telephone to her ear. She talks quietly, hoping, I suppose, that I can't hear.

'Louisa? That you? Put me through to the marshals' office right away.' There's a pause, then she says, 'Marshal Tate? I have got one of those *vick-ed* children from last night in the library right now . . . Good. See you in a moment.'

She replaces the telephone on its hooks, and I hurry back to my position, desperately scanning the room for an escape route. The librarian, unable, I guess, to contain her delight, is now talking to someone else, but all I hear is:

'I know . . . did you hear? Lucky to be alive . . . He was thrown clear of the crash . . .' Then, in a raised voice, 'With you in a minute, young man!'

'Okay! I mean . . . yes, all right!'

She obviously thinks she has me trapped without any means of getting away. And I think she may be right. Unless . . .

There's a long empty space on the shelf I'd been looking through. There's no back to the shelf, and it reveals the wall behind where there's a faded green sign. I can see the letters:

NCY

XIT

I remove a bunch of books to reveal the whole sign: EMERGENCY EXIT. The shelf has been built in front of the fire door! It really is my only hope. Curling my fingers round the shelf, I give it a sharp tug, and I feel it wobble. If it falls, it will expose the door, but it'll also crush me.

If I go to the end of the aisle to avoid the falling shelf, the librarian will surely see me. The words of a nursery rhyme that Dad used to sing to me drift into my head.

> 'We can't go over it . . .
> We can't go under it . . .
> We'll have to go through it!'

Through it? How on earth could I go . . .

I hear the librarian say, 'Goodbye,' and the click of the telephone being replaced, followed by the scraping sound of a chair being pushed back.

I look again at the space I've created on the shelf. It's about chest height. I'd be able to go through it. I grab the 2044 book and shove it down the front of my trousers.

I hear the librarian say, 'Now then, young man, I'll have you know I do not believe a . . . Oh my Lord. Stop it! That shelf isn't stable . . .'

With both my hands gripped round the back of the shelf, I give an almighty tug and it wobbles, then starts to topple. Books fall from the upper shelves on to the floor. I immediately plunge my head and shoulders into the gap and find the whole structure passing over me as it falls. I can see the fire door and its metal bar, and I hear the librarian scream, 'You vandal! You dreadful miscreant! My luffly books!'

I could not have anticipated the chaos that follows.

As the shelf that I'd pulled falls against the next shelf, its weight causes that one to topple as well, and the next one, like a stack of dominoes. Books are flying everywhere, and I push myself up through the gap and throw myself at the metal bar of the fire escape.

The door won't budge, so I try again. It might be decades – centuries even – since it was opened.

Frau Schwartz has hitched up her long skirt and is trying to climb over the collapsed shelving to get to me. 'You shall not get away, you wretch, you . . . you caitiff!'

You what? I throw myself at the door one last time as I'm hit on the head by a large hardback, and the door bursts open in a shower of dust, bugs and dry moss.

Stumbling through, I find myself in a narrow alleyway with the seafront to my right. I slam the door behind me and stagger along to the end, the muffled screams of the librarian following me. There I check both ways before emerging, and I hear a hiss.

'*Psst. Tommo. This way!*'

Kylie and Duke have left the shelter of the Watch Tower and crossed the road to my side. There's another gap between the houses a few metres further on, and I follow them there, walking so as not to attract any attention from the few people that are about.

Once round the corner, we run. I look back once and see a horseman in a sort of uniform pass by. He doesn't turn to look at us. 'Was that . . .?' I begin.

'A Brownie, aye,' says Duke, adding, 'one of the marshals. They keep order. Sort of. No one likes them, though. Best avoided. And there's a good chance that Pinker's paid 'em to nab us.'

Only two streets behind the seafront and we're already back in the overgrown streets and thick bush. When we know we're not being pursued, we stop behind a tumbledown petrol station where knee-high weeds grow through the concrete. I take the book out from my trousers and show it to Kylie. She bares her big teeth in a grin.

'Good work, mate!' She holds up her hand for a high-five and, when I respond, she grabs my hand and shakes it for a bit.

For a moment, it feels like we're already home and dry.

We hear the horses' hooves before we see the marshals.

CHAPTER 41

There are two mounted Brownies coming towards us. By the time they get near, all three of us are hiding inside the former petrol station, peeking through a long gap in the wall. The marshals are riding tall grey horses, and they're going quickly, looking from left to right, clearly searching for something – probably us. One of them is peering intently at the ground, studying the earth for any tracks we may have left. Where we left the road, he stops as his companion rides on.

Duke mutters a word under his breath that I don't understand. The Brownie dismounts for a better look at the dirt, then he squints exactly in our direction. He's just turned to call out to his mate when a pair of stray dogs come up behind him and start barking. His horse gets the jitters, and the Brownie grabs the reins to stop it bolting while kicking out at the dogs.

The other Brownie in the distance calls, 'Come on, man! It's just strays!'

He doesn't need more encouragement, and as the dogs

come back again, snarling, he remounts and gees on the horse with an angry, '*Hyah!*'

We wait until the sound of hooves has gone, and then we all breathe out at once.

'I need to pee,' says Duke, and he goes out through what was once the back door of the petrol station. A moment later, he reappears, smiling.

'There's a real khazi out there! Frogs living in it.' He sees our expressions. 'No – I did not pee on them. But I did find these.'

He tosses us each a plastic bottle of water and says, 'You folks left so much behind. There's still plenty to be found.'

Kylie examines the lid closely, then twists it off, cracking the seal. She sniffs it, then takes a long thirsty gulp and says, 'Well. It has to be better than cat food!'

We sit there for a few moments among the twenty-first-century leftovers. The fridges are stripped bare, and their filthy glass doors hang open; there's an ATM that – at some point in the past – someone has attacked with an axe or a sledgehammer, and tills almost invisible under centuries of accumulated dirt.

Duke drains the last of his water, burps loudly and says, 'So, Wonder-Age friends, how are we getting you back to 2023 then? Got any bona ideas? We gonna walk to Newcastle?'

'I . . . I cannot believe you seem so, well . . . relaxed,' says Kylie.

Duke stands up, stretches and sighs, looking into the distance as though wondering whether to say something. He pushes back his bowler hat and scratches his head. 'It's an act, Kylie. Have you ever heard that fing about faking a smile? That sometimes it turns into a real one? It's same-same with bravery. My uncle used to say—' He stops, bites his bottom lip, then starts again. 'My uncle says that pretending to be brave is very like really being brave. It's how I learned to deal with me stepfather. It's how I can stand up and prattle to a lotta people through a megaphone. Right now, I'm terrified. But that's not gonna bring Ocean back, is it? If I pretend to be brave, though, we just might.'

Kylie looks downcast. Perhaps she's thinking what I'm thinking: that there's no guarantee that this is even going to work. Kylie's 'forking destinies' theory is just that: a theory.

She says, 'I don't think I've ever had to be brave in my life. Not properly brave. I was scared coming to England, but all I had to do was sit on a plane.'

I'd never thought of Kylie being scared to come and live with us, and feel a slow smile spread over my face: a real one, not a fake one. I turn to my cousin. 'What about it, Kylie? Shall we pretend to be the world's bravest kids?' I stand and offer my hand to pull her up.

'Sounds okay to me, Tommo,' she says. She holds out her hand, and all three of us grip together.

'Home?' I say.

They repeat it. 'HOME!'

'We can't walk to Newcastle,' says Duke. 'There's only one road, plus the train-way. They'll bofe be patrolled by Brownies.' He points up the street. 'After here, it's just dense bush and flooding. We can't make it in time, and it's too dangerous anywhich, even with an axe.'

'So what do you suggest?' I say.

'We have to pretend to be brave,' he says. 'And that means going by the river. So first we gotta get to Nanny Moo's.'

An hour later, we arrive – via thickly wooded lanes and after a standoff with some more stray dogs – in Tynemouth. Like Culvercot, it's just about recognisable in its overall layout and shape. Most of the houses and shops – at least on Front Street – seem occupied, interspersed with entire ruined streets. There's a building halfway down the street that looks as though it's recently suffered a huge fire. We keep to the shadows of the bright morning, often splitting up into ones and twos so that anybody looking for 'three children' might not notice us. Our distinctive sweaters are probably a giveaway so we take them off, which is a relief because the day is getting very warm.

Prior's Park, the big green space where we hold our school summer carnival, now has one half of its area planted with trees – apples and pears free for the taking – and I'm so hungry I try one. It's unripe and sour. At the edge of the orchard, Duke holds up his hand to stop us, and we stay in the shade, looking down the bank to the river.

I ask the obvious question. 'Can we just walk along the riverbank – you know, all the way to Newcastle?'

Duke shakes his head. 'Not possible. Too overgrown. Vada there.' He nods upriver where the bushes grow down to the water's edge,

'Perhaps there's a ferry?'

'Eight a.m. and ten a.m.' He points at a big open-topped vessel with two large triangular sails, heading upriver. 'That was the ten a.m., I suppose.'

We go quiet for a while. Kylie says, 'Do you have any other ideas?'

'No – that was it. I fought we might risk it. You know – pretend to be brave and everyfin.'

'There's a difference between brave and reckless,' says Kylie. 'And, if marshals are watching everywhere, then I guess we have to keep out of sight.'

I feel like I've spent the whole of my life crouching behind things, concealing myself and generally hiding from unknown horrors, but it's actually only been a few hours. Still, here I am again, with Kylie and Duke, hunched over and heart thumping, behind a low wall, looking at a dirty whitewashed cottage that faces the harbour.

'If this is where we're headed, why are we hiding?' I whisper to Duke.

'I wanna be sure Nanny Moo's alone. You know – nobody waiting there for us . . . like that one, for example.'

He points at a marshal on a grey horse – a woman this time, dressed in brown – coming round the corner of the white cottage followed by an elderly woman in a long skirt, holding a tray of filleted fish. They exchange words as the old lady puts some fish in a plastic bag, which she offers up to the marshal. The marshal looks at the bag and shakes her head so the old lady adds some more fish. The marshal nods curtly, puts the fish package in a saddlebag and gallops off up the path away from the house. When she's out of sight, Duke stands up.

'You wait here,' he says, then he walks confidently towards the house.

Half a minute later, we hear the old lady's delighted shout from where we're hiding. Not long after comes Duke's loud finger-whistle, and now the three of us are inside the furniture-crammed cottage, and the old lady is dabbing her eyes and saying, 'But what about Ocean? What about my Ocean? Who are you?'

We try our best to explain what happened. But it's not an explanation that is easy to believe, however true it is. The old lady just looks bewildered, and I feel sorry for her.

We ask if the marshal had any news about Monsieur Lumière. Nanny Moo shakes her head sadly.

'That mob searched for him after the crash, but there

was no sign. They say he was thrown into the old quarry, though I don't know how that's even possible. I'm so sorry, Duke. Duke?'

Duke is staring out of the window. I'm not sure he's even heard what Nanny Moo said.

'That dog Pinker!' she spat. 'It's all his fault. And now the marshals have been telling me to report to them if you reappear. Can you get my Ocean back?' she says, her eyes brimming with tears once more.

'We'll try, Nanny Moo,' says Kylie. 'But we gotta get to Newcastle by eight o' . . . o' . . . oh my goodness me. Is that . . . is it . . .?' She points out of the window.

I don't think I've ever seen a less alive figure than the one who, right now, is staggering up the path towards us.

CHAPTER 42

If it wasn't for the clothes, I would not have recognised Monsieur Lumière.

His hair – surely a wig – sits on his head like a drowned black cat. His coat is soaked through and burnt, his face is covered in dirt and soot, and a huge gash in his trousers reveals a bloody wound on his thigh. He pauses to run a gloved hand over his forehead, and Duke rushes forward to throw his arms round this ghastly mess of a human. Silently, the two hug each other, and for a moment it doesn't seem right to interrupt them.

Yet it's almost magical to watch Monsieur Lumière's transformation: it's as though the embrace from Duke has been a life-restoring potion. Slowly, his stoop disappears, and his shuffling walk becomes stronger and steadier as he and Duke make their way towards the front door.

If Duke was delighted to see his uncle, Nanny Moo seems less so. As soon as he's within earshot, she barks, 'Where is she? Where's Ocean? What have you done with her?'

Monsieur Lumière puts his hands together as if in

prayer, wincing a little at his bad arm. 'My dear madame. If I am right, then she's not far in space. Only time separ-reparates us.'

'What on earth does that mean? Because the Brownies are out looking for her. And you. And these three. I'm harbouring wanted criminals, and—'

'Madame. Please. My belief is that they may well have been paid to find the Time Tablet.' He looks over to where Kylie has unwrapped it and is holding it up to him. 'I'm glad to see it is safe. For it may be the only means to bring Ocean back.'

'Strewth, mate,' says Kylie, eventually. 'We thought you were a goner.'

A puzzled look crosses Monsieur Lumière's blackened face. 'A goner?'

'We thought you were dead,' she says. 'Sorry, Dukoe, but we did.'

Monsieur Lumière gives Duke a final squeeze and says, '*Alors, mes amis*, you must tell me exactly what happ-appened. Where is Ocean?'

'You mean you don't know?' says Nanny Moo.

He doesn't answer. Instead, he staggers forward and collapses on to a wooden bench. With a sigh, Nanny Moo begins to fuss about him with clean cloths and bowls of water and fish broth.

'Ah, *soupe de poisson*,' he sighs as he sips the broth. 'Another signific-ificant French invention.'

Duke helps too, and I feel a bit useless, but I'm on my third mug of fish broth, which – I promise you – tastes much, *much* better than it sounds.

A little later, Monsieur Lumière reclines on the sofa in clean clothes, his thigh bound with a bandage, his arm in a new sling, and he's able to tell us his story.

'The exact moment the Wonderbuggy was about to crash into the train . . . ahh! I thought my life was termin-erminated. And then – *quel miracle!* – the belt of safety rips open, and I am thrown clear of the crash by the considera-bubble impact. The other driver? He 'ad jumped free long before, and there were no passengers aboard, thank 'eavens.

'Seconds later – *boum!* – the 'ole thing goes up in the sky as the fuel catches fire. I 'ad been thrown several metres and am lying, invisi-bubble and dazed, in the ditch. I am about to cry out 'elp me, 'elp me . . . and then I see him. That devilish beast of a man, Pinker! And I keep my 'ead down. And after that, well . . . I do not remember much because I pass out, there in the ditch. When I come round, it is light, and I make my way 'ere.'

He gazes up at us, and his eyes glisten with tears. 'I am so 'appy you are safe.' He then looks at Duke and nods slowly. '*Formidable*,' he says in French, adding in English, 'formida-bubble.'

'I'll give you formida-bubbly, you French fool,' says Nanny Moo, but not meanly. 'What were you thinking getting these children involved? And what about my Ocean?'

Monsieur Lumière struggles to his feet, clears his throat and straightens his shoulders. He grips the blanket that is round his shoulders with the hand in the sling and points up with his other hand, looking into the distance at an imaginary audience.

'Madame, messieurs, now is not the time for recriminim-inations. Let us consider instead our actions. For, right now, four 'undred and two years ago, Ocean Mooney is 'oping – along with our two friends 'ere – to return 'ome. Ah, 'ome . . . a word that warms the 'eart and—'

'Oh, stop it, you old show-off,' interrupts Nanny Moo. 'If it's as urgent as you say, then we need to get started. It's about time that son of mine made up for leaving me and his daughter alone, eh?'

'Your son, madame? I was not aware . . .'

'Well, shut your French *gâteau*-hole and become aware. Follow me.'

With trembling old fingers, Nanny Moo inserts a key into the rusty padlock that has been unopened, she says, for ten years. The boat-shed doors part with a creak. Inside is a long flat boat with a hinged mast lying along its length, its grey sail folded round it, on top of the wooden seats.

'This was Ocean's pa's?' gasps Duke, and she nods, looking a little sad. 'She never said!'

Nanny Moo says, 'She didn't even know. It was found capsized out by the Dogger Bank by some fishers from Blyth. No sign of him. They towed it all the way back. I didn't want Ocean to go to sea. I've known that heartbreak too often: a son, two brothers – all taken by the waves . . .'

Duke walks round the vessel, knocking it with his fist, kicking it. Monsieur Lumière, who was slower down the harbour steps, now approaches, looking proud. 'He knows a lot about boats, do you not, Duke?'

Duke leans on the vessel, which creaks in protest. 'I'd sooner forget every second I spent at sea. But I know a little. This is a *Nordlandsbot*, a poor one, made from pine. Popular in Norway, Scotland, Denmark. Not good for deep water, really, but . . .' He catches Nanny Moo's eye. 'I'm sure he knew what he was doing.'

'He was a very experienced sailor, my son,' she said firmly. 'But what about you, lad? Can you sail this thing upriver?'

'No. It's completely unseaworvy. The pine planks've shrunk from being so dry. Look: there are gaps everywhere. It'll sink in minutes. And there's a strong westerly wind meaning we'd never make it up the river in time anywhich.'

The glum silence that descends after Duke's little speech is thick, like a bank of fog. Duke says no more, but leaves the boat shed and walks down the gravel bank to the water's edge where he stands, his face turned to the wind, and appears to be taking deep breaths through his nose. He adjusts his hat, straightens his shoulders and seems to be muttering to himself.

'Wind's gonna turn in a few hours,' he says when he gets back. It's like he's suddenly in charge. He claps his hands and points to me. 'Get some wood tar, quickly. And, Kylie – fetch a mallet.'

'Some . . . what?' I say.

'What's a mallet when it's at home?' says Kylie. 'Is it something to eat cos I'm still starving?'

Duke rolls his eyes. 'We have six hours to make sure this boat doesn't sink wiv us in it.'

A mallet turns out to be a wooden hammer that we use to thump tiny pieces of wood into the gaps between the boat's planks. Once that's done, we flip it over and apply tar – a kind of sticky paint – to the hull for waterproofing. All the time, Nanny Moo is nervously watching for approaching marshals.

'I know all these people,' she says of the men and women coming and going in the harbour. 'Most of them are good. But five hundred crowns can easily turn a friend into an enemy.'

No one comes near. Nanny Moo brings down a huge plate of fried fish, which we devour behind the closed door of her boat shed. By 5 p.m., we're nearly finished.

The hull – not to mention our hands and clothes – is coated with sticky brown tar.

We turn the boat the right way up and make sure the hinged mast can be erected and the sail raised. We're filthy, sweaty, covered in wood tar and completely exhausted when Nanny Moo reopens the double doors of the shed. She glances around.

'All clear,' she says.

Monsieur Lumière stands up and faces us. 'My friends,' he starts, '*mes amis . . .*'

But no one listens because we're all tugging the boat across the pebbles and into the water. He stops speaking and hobbles after us.

'These boats ain't common around here,' says Duke, using a long pole to push away from the shore. 'Even among the other boats, we might attract looks, so keep your bonces down. Kylie, do you have the Time Tablet?'

She holds it up, tightly wrapped in plastic bags to stop it getting wet. We've already started to drift downriver – the opposite direction we need to go. Duke then hoists the sail up the mast, and it fills with the breeze.

'Wind's dropped,' he says. 'This is gonna take a while. There are five of us. It's slowing us.'

'Will we make it, Dukoe?' says Kylie, a distinct tremor in her voice. He doesn't answer, but releases a rope to bring the sail round.

'Boom!' he shouts, and we all duck as the wooden spar swings across.

'I dunno,' he says when we cautiously raise our heads again. 'We're just gonna have to pretend to be brave.'

CHAPTER 43

OCEAN

I just want to go home.

I do not think anybody – apart from Pierre perhaps – has slept much. The house now has so many people in it there are not enough chairs. Most seem to be policers, some in uniforms, some not. They are nicer than the marshals I am used to. There are two 'child welfare officers' and a 'senior health officer'. I lost track a while ago.

Outside are motorcars and trucks and people that Melissa says are from newspapers and television and 'websites', whatever they are. And yet more lights, all pointing at the house, even in the daytime.

Once I went to the window to look out. My scream brought Melissa rushing back in from the bathroom.

'What's wrong?' she asked. I was cowering behind the bed, pointing at the massive black spider about half a metre across that hovered outside the window. She sighed and snapped the drapes shut.

'Drone,' she said. Then she added gently, 'It's not alive, Ocean. It's . . . mechanical. It takes photographs.'

Still, they keep knocking on the door and putting notes through the oblong hole in it asking me to talk with them. Pierre has retreated to the bedroom that I slept in and does not seem keen to come out. I know exactly how he feels.

There is a cat somewhere as well, called Korky, but I think she has had enough and was last seen up a tree in the next garden.

I am sitting in the kitchen, holding a cup of something they call 'milk', but it comes from plants. It is horrible. Melissa has offered me some 'cereal', but I do not know what that is. I asked for some chocolate, but Melissa said she had none.

I remember the layout of the house from when Duke and I came to dig up the Time Tablet. I told this to a policer, but I am not sure he understood properly. The yew tree is not there yet, of course: just a big space next to a shed.

Upstairs, Melissa helps me dress in some jeans and a sweater with a zip that belonged to Thomas, and I sit on the bed and eat a bowl of some brown things that look like scabs soaked in more 'milk'. Then, with a policer called Jenny sitting at the end of my bed and Melissa holding my hand, people are brought in to speak to me, and I tell them the same things over and over again. Pierre watches it all with an ungruntled look on his face from high on a bookshelf. He has been given a bag of nuts, but he does not seem very hungry.

A young woman and man – 'digital investigations officers' – come in and ask the same questions and then look at Kylie's computer screens, tapping the keyboards quickly and confidently. The woman says to me, 'Do you know Kylie's password, Ocean?' and when I say no, she nods and has a murmured confab with her partner, none of which I understand.

They look closely at the Time Tablet as well, then she says, 'So tell me again. You say an exact copy of this "time tablet" exists in – what was it – the year 2425?'

'No,' I say. 'Not an exact copy. It is the same one. It was buried under the yew tree like I told you. The yew tree outside that isn't there yet. We found it.'

The officer says, 'So . . . you've been here before?'

I think about this for a moment. 'Well, before for me. Four hundred and two years after for you.'

'Impossible,' murmurs one of the officers, which crossens me. It is as though she is accusing me of lying.

'All right, if it is impossible, how do I know there is a green motorcar in the garage at the back? We saw it when we dug up the Time Tablet.'

This is a risk: I do not know for certain that it is there. Melissa nods at the policer. 'She's right. There is. Freddie's MGB's in there. We haven't mentioned it, and Ocean hasn't been out there.'

The officer sighs. 'It makes no sense. It can't be.'

'But it is,' I say. 'Nothing is impossible. Lots of things, however, are highly unlikely.'

There is a knock on the door. Freddie comes in with a laptop computer, opened up to show the screen, which he holds out to Melissa.

He says, 'So much for the news blackout. It's everywhere. Budge up, Ocean.'

He sits next to me and says, 'You're pretty famous, love. Everyone knows your story.'

'Everyone?' I say. 'Everyone in the world?'

He half laughs. 'Well, maybe not *everyone*. But what happened last night is news all round the world. On television, YouTube, websites, news media, radio . . .'

'But how?' I say. 'Is it the . . . internet?'

Of course, I have heard of the internet, also called the worldwide something-or-other, but I never really understood what it was.

Freddie thinks, then nods. 'Yup. I guess that's the simplest way of describing it.'

Melissa looks at the screen and makes the words on it roll up. There are pictures as well as words.

WHERE ARE THEY?
TV disappearance of computer kids sparks mystery

MONKEY BUSINESS
**Is this the moment future experiment
went wrong?**

SATURDAY NIGHT FAKE-AWAY
**Geordie duo's show blasted as 'sick
joke' by MP**

THE KID WHO CAME FROM SPACE
**Ocean, 11, and monkey are
'extraterrestrials' says ex-NASA boffin**

COULD YOU BE A TIME TRAVELLER?
Click here to find out

Freddie holds up his cellphone. 'You're the number-one trending topic on Twitter. Hashtag future girl, hashtag Andy & Des. I've had to shut off my Facebook, Insta, everything.'

(I do not know what any of this means. This is like a different language.)

'You might like this, though,' he says. 'It's on TikTok.' He holds his cellphone out to me and touches the screen. I watch in astonishment as Pierre appears, falling out of the Time Tablet in front of Kylie and Thomas. One of the men – Andy or Des – says, 'Whoa! Check it out!' and then the clip repeats, and jerks about and spins, all accompanied by a song going *'Monkey business, check-it-out check-it-out, do your monkey business!'* I play it again instantly, and then yet again.

Melissa presses the keyboard, and a film starts on the screen. A woman is holding a black stick by her chin and talking. Behind is the house I am in right now. I can even see my bedroom window with the closed drapes.

'As everybody knows by now, the mystery surrounding the two children, Thomas Reeve and his cousin Kylie Woollagong, began last night live on BBC television when a light-hearted look at a 13-year-old's invention took a very dark turn, beginning with the appearance of a monkey, seemingly from out of the screen of a tablet computer, followed by a young girl.

'Nobody seems sure at this point if the whole thing was – and remains – an elaborate illusion designed to fool the world. Celia Taylor, the producer of the show that stars TV favourites Andy and Des, insists that what we all saw was real, and that neither she nor Andy and Des have any knowledge of where Thomas and Kylie might be. She has been taken into custody and is helping the police with their enquiries. Andy and Des have issued a statement saying they are deeply concerned and are cooperating fully with the investigation.

'Meanwhile, the girl who appeared out of the screen has told investigators her name is Ocean Mooney, that she was born in the year 2413 and that the monkey belongs to a Monsieur Mustapha B. Lumière, a travelling showman. She is being interviewed by investigators at this house behind me in Culvercot, Tyneside.

'It all sounds very unlikely, but one thing is clear. If this is indeed an elaborate deception, then the joke has worn thin pretty quickly. This is Jaimie Bates for WorldCom News in Tyneside.'

The tears falling on to the laptop's keyboard turn out to be mine. I had not even realised I was crying, but all of this attention, the questions, the noise . . .

It goes on for hours.

Later, Freddie asks me if I am hungry and I say, 'Do you have pizza?'

He laughs and says, 'Only frozen, I'm afraid.'

He opens a cupboard that wisps of smoke come from and removes a flat box containing a small pizza that is frozen solid. He puts this into another little cupboard and pushes a button. A few minutes later, the machine goes 'ping' and the pizza is hot.

The Wonder Age indeed. I wonder, as I bite into the scalding pizza, if I will ever leave.

CHAPTER 44

At some point in the afternoon, I lie on my bed in the warm arms of Melissa. I do not know when the others leave the room or how long I am there, crying for myself, for Nanny Moo, for Duke and the others, but, when I open my eyes again and take a deep sniff, there is only me, Melissa (who appears to be asleep) and Pierre who stares up at me with his big green eyes, resting his little hand on mine. The clock on the desk says seven fifteen and I am suddenly wide awake. I nudge Melissa to awaken her.

'We have forty-five minutes,' I tell her, sitting up straight. 'What are we going to . . .'

Just then, Freddie comes in with a man with short grey hair in a policer's uniform with lots of gold braid, badges and colours sewn on to it. He looks important. Surely I am going home?

'Hello, Ocean,' the man says gruffly. 'My name's Nelson Nkolo. I'm the Chief Constable for Northumbria Police.'

Freddie chips in. 'He's the Big Boss.'

The man smiles coldly and joins us sitting on the bed. He clears his throat.

'When I was your age, Ocean, I arrived in a chilly and rainy England from a hot and sunny Zambia. Do you know where that is?'

I shake my head. He sounds as though he has practised saying all of this.

'It doesn't matter. It's far away. Anyway, as soon as I got here, all I wanted to do was go home. My mum and dad were still in Zambia, you see; I was living with my aunty and uncle, and I was so unhappy. Everything was so different. The weather, the food, the way people spoke, the way people looked, the cars in the streets, the shows on television . . .'

He is being kind, and he has a nice face. So why am I feeling that this is going to take a wrong turn?

'Now we don't know where you've come from . . .'

'I have told you!'

'Yes. Well. You see, I know what it's like to be alone in a strange place. I want to help you, Ocean. Like I say, we don't know *exactly* where you've come from. But don't worry – we will find out. Likewise, the whereabouts of Kylie and Thomas – that is under the most urgent investigation. In the meantime . . .'

I can feel myself getting scared, for this is heading where I feared it might. I interrupt. 'I have told you where they are as well. We swapped places! The Time Tablet did it!'

The man blinks and cocks his head a little towards me. It is a tiny movement, but it says, *Steady on. I'm losing patience with this Time Tablet business.*

He clears his throat again. 'Quite. You have said so, and your story's commendably consistent. I want to reassure you, Ocean, that we take your well-being, and that of Kylie and Thomas, very seriously indeed. That is why I'm permitting you to stay here with Mr and Mrs Reeve. You'll be quite safe. There will be a permanent patrol car outside the house.'

He picks up the Time Tablet and looks at it, then hands it to me. 'Ocean, this is a toy. It can't possibly do what you say. The sooner you admit that, the better for everyone, I think. There's some serious investigating to be done around this case, but talk of time travel, and future worlds, and meteorites in twenty forty something . . .'

'Twenty forty-four! In . . . in America somewhere.' Then I repeat the rhyme that we all know from when we were little:

'In twenty hundred and forty-four
The population grew no more . . .'

He shakes his head sadly. 'We'll get to the bottom of what's going on with you, Ocean.'

That cannot be happening. 'No! I need to be there at eight o'clock tonight! Otherwise I cannot get back, and what happened to my world will happen to yours!'

I am shouting now, but this man looks like he is used to staying calm when people shout at him.

'*You saw it all!*' I scream. 'It has been all over your stupid televisions and computer thingies and . . . and . . . mobile phone-cells. Everyone has seen it! How can you not believe it?'

'And, once we've discovered the truth, they will believe that too. I'm sorry you're upset, Ocean, but that's how it is.'

Throughout this exchange, I have half noticed that Freddie has been getting impatient, his foot tapping on the bedroom carpet. Now he stands up and says, 'Come off it, Chief Constable. You can't just dismiss what she said as easily as that.'

Oh, thank you, Freddie! It is such a relief that *someone* believes me.

Freddie goes on, 'Let's at least give her a chance to prove she's telling the truth. She said eight p.m. That's not long now.'

The police chief stands up as well. 'I'm sorry, Mr Reeve. I'm sorry, Ocean, but you must stay here for your own safety. That's my decision. Good evening to you all.'

He turns to leave, with Freddie following him. I hardly see them go because my eyes are misted with tears, but I hear the bedroom door click shut, like someone is turning a lock on the rest of my life. I hear raised voices on the landing and all the way down the stairs, Freddie yelling, 'Flamin' useless flamin' idiots! We pay our taxes, you know! Why don't you try doing some proper policing for a change?' Then the front door slams.

Peeking out between a gap in the drapes, the road outside is fuller than ever as a police car pulls away with the Chief Constable in it. There are vans with big dish-shaped things on them, and people holding microphones (I guess) and talking to huge cameras on tripods, and other people who seem to have just come along to look at the house. Then, from somewhere – I cannot tell where – there is a low thumping noise: *dup dup dup dup dup.* Looking into the sky, I see what I think is a helicopter or some other sort of aerialplane, black and hovering. Then it circles out of sight before returning 'gain.

If only Monsieur Lumière could see, I think, before stepping back from the window and slumping down on the bed. The clock on the wall reads 7.29 p.m.

I am never going to see my home again. Not Nanny Moo, not Monsieur Lumière, not Duke . . .

There is a tap at the door, and Freddie puts his head round. He jingles something metal in his hand and says, 'Wanna ride, Ocean?'

'A ride? In what?'

'What do you think? My sports car!' He smirks for

some reason I do not get. 'It's not a DeLorean, but there's a chance you could go back to the future.'

Then he outlines a plan that is so daring I feel sick. But it is the only plan we have.

I look at the clock: 7.32 p.m.

CHAPTER 45

THOMAS

Once past the mouth of the river, our progress has been good, even though the boat immediately began letting in water through the cracks. The wind picked up by the time we got to Wallsend, and, after skilful sailing from Duke, and steady bailing from the rest of us, we can see the outskirts of Newcastle as we round the bend of the Tyne. According to Monsieur Lumière's watch, we still have half an hour to spare.

In fact, I've almost forgotten that it's possible – unlikely, but possible – that Pinker will have worked out our plans from the instructions dropped on the church floor.

'Oh my word, Tommo – check out the bridge!' says Kylie.

About half a kilometre ahead of us is the unmistakable crescent shape of the Tyne Bridge, except a portion of the road section is missing, replaced by . . . what? It's hard to see.

'Halt!' calls Monsieur Lumière from the front of the boat. 'And get down.'

We all obey. Duke releases the boom, and the sail goes limp. Almost immediately, the boat starts to drift downriver. Monsieur Lumière takes a rusty telescope from the boat's locker and trains it on the bridge. Then he too ducks.

'*Zut alors!*' he spits. 'It is as we feared. Pinker is there along with some others. They are gathered on the north side.'

While we were preparing the boat, we'd come up with a plan of sorts. I did not – and still don't – think it'll work. But, seeing as I couldn't think of anything better, I kept quiet.

Monsieur Lumière outlines again what we're about to do. '*Écoutez.* Pinker and his confeder-ederates are on the north side of the bridge. So – we approach from the south. We must get to the centre of the bridge without being noticed. It will take Pinker a few moments to reach us, even if he sees us. Then he 'as to get over the rope bridge, which takes longer. We will be done by then.'

We're all silent. Then Kylie says, 'Is that it then? That's the plan? Listen, guys: I've seen movies, right? I've read stories.' She catches me looking wide-eyed. 'Okay, not many. But enough to know that in a situation like this we need a massive distraction, like setting something on fire. Or . . . or a secret weapon. Or a cunning disguise? What I mean is – we're just *walking*? And then hoping for the best? Can't we do any better than that?'

You see, put like that, I think Kylie's got a point. All the bravery I'd built up – even if it was fake – drains away in that instant, and I'm actually furious with her as a result. It's like I had a sink full of courage, and Kylie has just reached in with her big, stupid Australian arm and yanked out the plug.

Even in the few moments that we've stopped, we have drifted quite a way downriver and the water in the boat's hull now laps over our feet. Eventually, Duke raises his hand. 'I'll do it,' he says, swallowing hard.

'You'll do . . . what?' says Kylie.

'You're right. I'll distract them. Leave it to me.'

He's already on his feet, pulling at the sail to make it catch the wind. Straight away we stop drifting and start heading for the opposite shore.

'Duke, Duke, my boy – what do you mean?' says Monsieur Lumière, his good fist clenched in anxiety. 'You cannot—'

'I can,' says Duke, his jaw set firm. He doesn't look round. 'I know Pinker far too good. I know exactly how to angerfy him. Just long enough to buy ye some time. Just long enough for him to . . .' He tails off as he expertly steers the boat next to a rough jetty.

'To what?' says Kylie. 'To . . . to *beat* you?'

Duke turns his head, and I can see the fear etched in his face. 'Some fings are worth it if it gets Ocean back.'

I start to say, 'It may not even work,' but Kylie pokes me in the back, and I shut up. Duke doesn't notice.

He says, 'Go on now – you ain't got much time. Two tacks should get ye to the other side.'

He leaps on to the jetty and pushes the boat away with his foot.

'Duke! No!' shouts Kylie. But Duke stays standing there, and he's actually *grinning*.

'It's all right!' he shouts with a wave of his bowler hat. 'I ain't really brave – I'm just pretending!' Then he turns and runs up the jetty on to the shore.

Nanny Moo navigates the boat towards the south bank of the river, between two larger fishing vessels, a good way downriver of the bridge. If the gang on the bridge have noticed the unusual vessel, then they surely can't recognise us? That is what I'm hoping.

There aren't many people around. A small flock of geese is being herded by a dog and its owner on to a horse-drawn cart, and a few fishermen are loading up empty crates. Other than that, the south quay is almost empty.

Kylie looks around nervously. 'I don't like this, mate,' she says with uncharacteristic gloominess. 'We'll stick out a mile.'

Monsieur Lumière overhears. 'But this is good news. Look.'

He breaks off from mooring the boat to a rusty capstan to point up at the bridge. Two people holding a heavy basket between them are tottering across what I now see is a roped section suspended between the two broken halves.

'The more people on the bridge when we do our busi-nisiness, the better, *non*? We will blend in. And now pass me the axe. Let us go!'

If Monsieur Lumière was scared, it certainly wasn't showing. Perhaps he, too, has learned the secret of pretending to be brave. Nanny Moo, on the other hand, looks as though she might actually be sick. She's turned an odd shade of grey-green, and her mouth is puckered so tight that her lips have turned white. She doesn't meet our eyes.

'Good luck,' she mutters. 'I'm staying here to mind the boat. I'll sail it nearer in case . . . well, just in case.' The poor woman is panting hard, and puts her hand on her chest. She takes a few deep breaths.

Kylie takes a step towards her. 'Are you okay, Nanny Moo?'

I see her lips tighten again. 'I'm fine,' she says, obviously lying. ''Cept my granddaughter's stuck four hundred years in the past. The next five minutes depend on bravery: real lion-hearted courage.' Then she looks at us both, and

I see the fear and hope in her face. 'I hope you've got some.'

We climb the stone steps and muddy bank that go from the quay up to the start of the road that leads on to the bridge.

At the other end of the bridge, maybe three hundred metres away, I can see Pinker and his gang standing next to their horses, stopping a small crowd of people from walking across. Kylie hands me the package, and we unwrap the Time Tablet carefully before placing it back in the bag.

'Everything good?' I ask. She checks the wires and nods. The Haribo glue has held firm.

'We're going home, Kylie!' I say. I mean to sound confident, but I croak too much with nerves.

'Yeah, about that . . .' says Kylie, chewing her lip the way she does when she's nervous.

'What? Look, I know it might not work. You don't have to—'

'It's not that. It's just, well . . . there's no guarantee that everything will be the same if we get back?' She corrects herself quickly. '*When* we get back, I mean.'

'In what way?' I say, trying to sound as if this is a normal conversation.

'I dunno, mate. But we've already messed with space-time? Our future may not be the same as it would have been.'

'Isn't that a good thing?' I say. I tap my pocket where I have the page torn from the history book. 'We're going to prevent a catastrophe!'

Before Kylie can answer, we both hear, from the other side of the bridge, a scream like no other I have ever heard. It's not a scream of pain: just an animal howl. There's Duke, yelling his head off, and running in front of the group of people. *What is he doing?* Whatever it is, they're certainly not watching us as Monsieur Lumière pops open his pocket-watch and announces, 'Seven fifty-four, *mes amis*. From now on, our fate is not in our 'ands. Let us go.'

There's not even time for a deep breath, or a *good luck, everybody*. Instead, we walk towards the centre of the bridge as fast as Monsieur Lumière's bad leg will allow. It's not much of a plan, to be honest. All we're hoping is that we get there before Pinker notices.

Looking ahead, I see Duke kick Pinker hard in the shin and then run to one side of the bridge, dodging his outstretched arms, but careful not to direct his attention straight ahead where he might see us.

We're a quarter of the way over the bridge. That's almost halfway to the rope section. I can see where it's attached to the existing bridge by four thick ropes.

Duke has been caught by Pinker, who – furious at Duke's interruption – grabs him by the throat and delivers a powerful punch to Duke's abdomen, making him collapse on the ground. I pick up my speed. 'No, do not run,' says Monsieur Lumière. 'It only attracts attention. So far, we 'ave not been noticed.'

'So far' doesn't last long. He's hardly finished his sentence when three things happen at once.

1. I hear the bell of the clock of the old cathedral begin to strike eight.
2. The Time Tablet starts to glow at the bottom of the carrier bag.

And three? Three is the worst of all.

3. A large figure with a black beard has given up bullying a skinny boy. Pinker has mounted his horse and is spurring it on to gallop towards us.

CHAPTER 46

OCEAN

Freddie grips the car keys in his fist as he heads downstairs, with me and Pierre following a couple of paces behind. The Time Tablet and all its workings are concealed in my front smock pocket, bumping against my thighs as I walk.

In the living room are two policers, a man and a woman, sitting on the sofa, drinking tea with Melissa when Freddie and I enter. They both smile at me and the woman says, 'Hello, love. You feeling better?'

I glance at Freddie, then say the words he told me.

'I think I need some fresh air.'

Melissa says, 'It's crazy out the front. Why don't you take Ocean into the back garden, Freddie? More tea, officers?'

'Oh, good idea,' Freddie says as though he had not already thought of it.

'Is there any more cake?' says the man officer, smiling at Melissa, but barely looking at me.

I hardly recognise the garden, especially without the enormous yew tree. Still, the space where it grew is there, and next to it the shed where Duke found the axe. Only this time it has a roof, and the walls have not sunk inwards.

'Come on,' says Freddie. 'We have to be quick. Are you ready? Pierre – you coming too?'

Seconds later, we are inside, sitting low down in a shiny green motorcar without a roof. Pierre crouches warily on a little low shelf behind the two front seats. Freddie presses a button on something attached to the key, and a wide door in front of us begins to rise up as if by magic. He reaches over to me and pulls a strap round my chest, then turns the key in a slot. The car roars to life as a man with a camera peers into the garage.

I hear him say, 'Hey! She's in here!' and two other people with cameras start the whole flashing, clicking business.

'Hang on tight, Ocean,' Freddie says, although there is nothing to hang on to. The engine growls like an angry wolf, its long nose edges out of the garage and Freddie turns the wheel sharply to the right and into the back lane. The cameramen are leaning right over us, flashing their devices in our eyes, until Freddie presses the middle of the wheel he steers with and a loud *PAAAAAR!* makes them jump back in fright.

I am thrown right back into my seat when the car makes a massive surge forward, and the engine starts to scream rather than growl.

'Ha *haaaah!*' shouts Freddie, grinning and widening his eyes like a crazy man. At the end of the lane, he turns another sharp left, and then another till we are on a wider road where there are other cars. For about a half a minute, we have to slow down because there is too much "traffic" to move fast, and Freddie is saying, 'Come on, come on,' through his teeth. Then he stops completely in front of a red light. He honks his car horn to make it turn green, and we are off again. Soon there are fewer cars, and we are on a big wide road.

'Okay, Chitty, let's see what you're made of,' says Freddie, to the car, I think, and once again I am pressed back into my seat as Chitty goes faster and faster.

There is a clock in the front bit of the car. It now says 7.42 p.m.

Freddie parps the car's horn 'gain and 'gain. We are passing the other cars quickly, and as we do there is a noise like *zzim . . . zzim.*

'Outta the way! Outta the way!' shouts Freddie. Then, 'Oh sh— shoot.' He glances at me.

A noise comes from behind: the same wailing I had heard last night when we were in the police car. I turn in my seat to see two of them with flashing blue lights coming up behind us.

Suddenly, as though from nowhere, a motorcycle with two riders is 'longside us. The front person, his whole head covered in a shiny round ball, is hunched over the controls. Behind him, another rider has a camera and is leaning out, trying to get pictures of us.

'Flamin' paparazzi!' shouts Freddie, and he swerves a little to the left, causing the motorcycle to swerve too. Then it wobbles, and suddenly it is skidding along on its side, throwing the two riders clear. I look behind again, scared that they might be hurt, but I see them both stand up, and one of the police cars has stopped to check on them.

The other one has not, though. It is a fast car, and its siren is screaming, but still it has not caught up with us. Freddie moves the stick that is between the two seats, the engine's pitch changes, and we are going faster still, if that was even possible.

'Come *oooon*!' *Yee-haah!*' he shouts. I glance at him, and there is a manic look in his eyes, which I do not really like. I think he forgets that I have never in my life travelled this fast. And then, when I look ahead, there are more blue lights flashing, and Freddie mutters, 'Shoot,' again. The other cars on the road are slowing down. The police car behind us is very close, and then it is alongside us, next to Freddie, and the officer inside is gesturing angrily at him.

'No way, Jose,' says Freddie, who must know him somehow.

We are still going fast when I see his right foot move and press hard on a pedal that makes me jerk forward in my seat, and poor Pierre too, who hits the back of my seat with a thump. We have come to a complete halt very quickly indeed, and the police car alongside us has zipped ahead. Freddie moves the stick again and, with a screaming of smoking tyres and a whining of the engine, we are now going backwards, leaving the bunched-up cars and causing the vehicles that are coming towards us to swerve and honk their horns.

The police car that was chasing us is now trapped in the middle of about twenty other cars. More stick manoeuvres from Freddie, a turn to the left and we are on a different road and picking up speed again towards a red light. Instead of stopping, this time Freddie makes the car go even faster. We roar across a crossing of two roads, and I swear the car leaves the ground, to the sound of more squealing wheels, parping horns and something that sounds like two or more cars crunching together behind us.

Amid the noise, I hear a tinkling tune come from where Freddie is sitting and I already recognise this as the sound of a cellphone. He takes his hand off the driving-wheel and pulls the phone from his back trouser pocket, making the car swerve violently.

He looks at it then tosses it to me. 'Answer that for me will you?'

The screen is flashing the name MELISSA. 'Just, just . . . press the green dot! Mel? Mel? We're fine, we're . . . *get out of the way, you idiot!*' The car swerves again. 'No, not you, love!' Freddie is shouting to make himself heard above the roar of the car's engine. 'Meet us at the Tyne Bridge. We're gonna get them back Mel!'

The screen in my hand goes blank and I plunge my

hands deep in my smock's front pocket, hunching myself up in fear as we go faster yet.

The clock says 7.58 p.m. The road ahead is clear of other vehicles as it dips down under another road, into a short tunnel, and when we emerge I can see the huge Tyne Bridge looming ahead of us, all clean and 'luminated.

I gasp and clutch the Time Tablet closer. The bridge is awesome: pale blue-painted steel, a massive curve over the river. As we get nearer, I notice two helicopters hovering, one of them very low, almost touching the top curve of the bridge, like a huge black hornet waiting for us.

In seconds, we are driving across the bridge.

Then Freddie slows the car right down. Ahead of us are six police cars, stopped crossways on the road, their blue lights flashing, preventing any cars passing. We are behind about six other cars and a large van that have also had to stop. Looking behind us, where we joined the bridge, there are more blue lights. The bridge is blocked off at both ends, with only our car and a few other vehicles, all now at a standstill.

Two burly policers are ambling towards us.

'How's it looking?' murmurs Freddie to me, watching the policemen get closer. 'Because, you know, whether or not this works, I am in so much trouble you wouldn't believe. I'd just like to think it was worth it. Do you need to get out of the car to do this?'

'It is probly better.'

Freddie leans over and pulls a handle, opening the car door, and clicks a button to release the strap.

I see the long hand of the car's clock touch twelve. At exactly the same time, a distant clock starts to chime, and the screen of the Time Tablet in my hands begins to glow with its creamy-white ripples.

I swallow hard. 'Are you ready, Pierre?'

Time Tablet in one hand, monkey's paw in the other, I push open the car door and step out.

The policers are still advancing. 'Stand back!' I shout. 'Or I, the monkey and the Time Tablet are going over the side and into the water!'

Of course, I would not do any such thing. But they do not know that.

'All right, love. Calm down, calm down!'

'Not one step further, mind!' I say, stepping closer to the waist-high barrier at the side of the bridge. The drivers and passengers of the other cars have got out as well, or are watching us through their car windows.

I place the glowing Time Tablet on the ground, still keeping a guardy eye on the policers. I test it by dipping my hand into the screen, as though I am testing the temperature of water.

'All right, Pierre. You go first!'

And he does.

CHAPTER 47

THOMAS

We have started to run now.

BONG! goes the cathedral clock.

BONG!

'We cannot outrun the 'orse,' says Monsieur Lumière breathlessly. 'But we can stop 'im crossing the rope bridge.'

BONG!

BONG!

As he limps the final few metres, he reaches behind his back and swings the axe into both of his hands, lifting it over his head even before he stops moving. The sling that was supporting his damaged arm hangs loose from his neck.

BONG!

BONG!

I look down in dismay to see the light on the Time Tablet has gone out by the time the clock has finished its eighth chime. 'Kylie, Kylie – look! What's happening?'

BONG!
BONG!

On the other side of the rope bridge, Pinker's horse rears up at the bridge's broken edge. He leaps down and takes the first step on to the wobbly planks at the same moment that Monsieur Lumière brings the axe down on to the first of the arm-thick ropes that attach it to our side.

It makes a small incision, but nothing more. Pinker can see this, and, in his arrogance, he even stops after a few paces, each hand holding a rope on either side.

He yells across the gap. 'You're too late, Lumière! Always too late, ha? I'll 'ave that Time Tablet from you like I always knew I would.'

Monsieur Lumière delivers another blow to the rope, shouting, 'Owww!' with the pain this causes his injured arm. This blow cuts deeper, but still not deep enough. He stops to shout back at the figure on the rope bridge.

'Just let them go 'ome, Pinker! Let the children go, and you can 'ave it.'

'Oho, no! I know your game. There's a good chance the tablet and everything inside it will be useless if they use it again. No, no, Lumière! The Time Tablet an' silicon chip that goes with it are mine! To hell with the children!'

He starts moving quickly now, and the axe is brought down again along with a howl of agony from Monsieur

Lumière. One more blow should do it. Pinker's face registers fear, and I see he looks down at the river thirty metres below. He's only a few strides from our side when the final swing of the axe severs the left-hand rope, making the bridge suddenly lose tension on one side. Pinker grips the other side with both hands while the rope bridge swings alarmingly. But his feet remain on the planks as he edges yet closer.

'What's happened to the tablet, Kylie?' I gasp in terror. 'Why isn't it working?'

She takes it out of the bag and turns it over. 'It's a connection. One of the wires is loose. It was only held on with flippin' chewed-up sweets.' She holds it out to me. 'Here,' she says. 'Spit on it!'

'Spit on it? Why?'

'We've got to soften the sugar paste again, and I'm so scared I've got no spit. My mouth's as dry as a wombat's . . .'

She doesn't finish because I've gathered up some saliva and lobbed it right on the screen. 'Good shot,' sighs Kylie as she scoops it up and smears it into a blob of dried Haribo.

I hardly dare look back to the rope bridge. Pinker is nearly across, inching his way along the planks, some of which are now coming loose and tumbling down into the water below. The second rope is proving even harder to cut than the first. No wonder Monsieur Lumière is weakening. He's certainly panting and sweating with the effort.

Pinker's face is scarlet with fury and determination. He could almost leap the final metre or two, but that would mean letting go of the rope.

With a final stroke of the axe, and a groan of agony from Monsieur Lumière, the rope pings apart, the recoil from the nearest strand springing back and sending the axe spinning from his hands and on to the bridge. At the same time, there's a grunt of terror from Pinker as the sides of the rope bridge collapse, and he disappears from view.

I can't bear to watch him fall. I turn away, expecting to hear a splash, but the water's too far below.

Nor can I bear to watch Kylie, her hands trembling with fear, trying to mould the sticky ball of sugary gum around a protruding wire.

'Relax, Kylie. Take it easy. He's gone,' I say.

The news barely seems to register with her. Monsieur Lumière has turned towards us, panting and groaning with pain, his back to the now-destroyed rope bridge.

'That's it, that's it,' says Kylie, almost to herself. She takes her hand away from the wire, and it stays in place. As soon as she does this, the screen on the tablet starts to glow whiter and whiter, and she places it on the ground, her hands clasped in front of her as though in prayer. As we watch, the screen bulges outwards as if pushed from beneath.

'Oh please, oh please,' I hear myself muttering.

A tiny paw bursts through the surface, followed by the whole of a monkey falling upwards. 'Pierre!' shouts Monsieur Lumière as Pierre shoots up out of the misshapen screen and throws his arms round Monsieur Lumière's neck. 'Ah, *mon ami! Mon ami!* It is so good to see you. But – where is Ocean?'

'Oh my Lord,' I gasp, 'look out!' Behind Monsieur Lumière, Pinker is hauling himself over the edge of the broken bridge, grabbing the axe in one hand. He embeds the blade in the cracked bridge road and uses it to pull himself up further.

'Too flamin' late for your little Ocean, Lumière!' roars Pinker, standing up and taking a step towards us. We all cower back. He sneers and extends two palms, bloody from rope-burns. 'Seems like I hung on tighter than you expected, eh? Seems like I don't give up, don't it? Well, nor would you if you 'ad the Time Tablet within sight.'

'Stop!' yells Kylie. 'Don't you realise it's useless? After tonight, you won't be able to use it again for hundreds of years. Till the next solar megastorm!'

Pinker laughs: a booming but mirthless chuckle after which everything seems to go quiet.

'Ah, Kylie Woollagong, I presume? That was good work you did back then in twenty-whatever. Good work, sweet'eart, but a little primitive – depending on megastorms an' so on. Look around – amid all this destruction, our thinking ain't completely stopped. We're not savages, are we? You think I'm just some dumb sailor, eh? Is that what Duke told you? Thing is, that's only 'alf the story. An' now? Well, put it this way, if I 'ave that Time Tablet, an' the silicon chip inside it, then I can recreate the Wonder Age, can't I? I might very well be the greatest humanitarian ever to live. But not, of course, if you two go back an' destroy it all. So – just 'and it over like a good little girl, eh? It's for your own good.'

'You're lying!' screams Kylie. 'You're no humanitarian! You're just a vicious bully. Besides, you can let us go and you'll still have the Time Tablet.'

Pinker drums his fingers on his chin in a pantomime of someone thinking hard. Then he says, 'I've thought about it and . . . nope. That's simply not a chance I'm willing to take, is it? Thing is, I'm not interested in no muddlin' *time travel*.' Pinker sneers the words in a baby-voice. 'That's for your century and your stupid obsession wi' space ships and star wars. No – I'm interested in *right now*. I'm interested in the contents of that Time Tablet and I'm not gonna let you go back in time an' ruin it.'

I glance behind. Two more horsemen are galloping towards the southern approach to the bridge, putting an end to any thought I had of just, you know, picking up the Time Tablet and making a run for it.

The tablet is still on the ground a few metres in front of me. Three steps and I'll be on top of it and able to step through the glowing screen and be back in 2023.

I could do that. We could both do that. I look over at Kylie. She seems frozen with fear. Pinker moves to pick up the Time Tablet.

'You will get that tablet over my dead body!' yells Monsieur Lumière, stepping between Pinker and the glowing device.

'Oh yeah? Well, that can be arranged,' snarls Pinker. He lifts the axe to shoulder height and swings it down. Monsieur Lumière, still holding Pierre, leaps out of the way, but not fast enough: the blade catches him hard in his left ankle, causing him to howl with pain and crumple to the ground, groaning and still clutching Pierre.

'Oops, sorry – I missed,' says Pinker. 'Missed your damn throat!'

He lifts the axe again, but doesn't notice Pierre. The monkey leaps up from Monsieur Lumière's arms, and throws himself at Pinker's neck, teeth bared. Pinker screams and steps back, dangerously close to the edge of the broken bridge, but then he staggers forward again, dropping the axe so that he can put his big hands round Pierre's throat. Immediately, Kylie runs forward and kicks the axe off the edge, where it drops into the river below.

She turns to me. 'Promise me you'll come straight after me, Tommo? Goodbye, Monsieur Lumière. And Pinker? You can go and . . .' Her last words are inaudible as she steps into the glowing light of the Time Tablet.

I say, 'Good lu—'

She's gone. I'm about to follow her when Pinker manages to throw Pierre off just far enough so that he can stagger to his feet and reach for the Time Tablet. I dash forward, foot poised to step into the light, but Pierre is back, darting between us and taking the tablet in both hands. He leaps on to the side of the bridge, out of reach of either of us.

'No, Pierre!' I shout, terrified that he'll drop the tablet into the river and end forever my chance of getting home. Using his legs while his arms clutch the tablet, the monkey starts to shin up one of the uprights that connect to the huge arch of the bridge, taking him higher and higher.

'Well, that changes things, don't it?' growls Pinker.

CHAPTER 48

OCEAN

The second after Pierre disappears into the screen of the Time Tablet, there is an audible gasp from the onlookers. Now the honking of car horns on the bridge has stopped as people all around us have got out of their cars. The only noises are the helicopters above us, the final clock chimes from the cathedral and a squawking kittiwake disturbed from its roost on the bridge's girders.

The policers are joined by more uniformed people, and I fear I am going to be overwhelmed. Freddie is at the front of the gathering crowd, arms spread out, shouting, 'Leave her! Leave her alone! I want my son back!'

'Come on, Ocean – hand it over. It's for your own good,' says a familiar voice. I look up and the crowd of uniforms parts to allow through Chief Constable Nkolo who had sat with me on the bed. He reaches out as if he is going to pick it up but I get there first.

'No!' I say. 'One more step . . .' I make as though I

am about to cast the Time Tablet over the side of the bridge, and he stops.

'You're getting yourself into more trouble, Ocean,' he says.

'Is that so?' I say, and I cannot believe I am being so bold. 'I am stuck four hundred and two years in the past! How much more trouble can I be in? Do you want Thomas and Kylie to come back? Well, stay right where you are!'

I replace the Time Tablet on the ground and, as soon as I do, the light fades and goes out. My heart sinks. What is going on? I nudge it with my foot.

All around me, the people who have got out of their cars are holding their cellphones in front of their faces. Another police car has pulled up behind the crowd, and I see Melissa get out of the rear door and rush forward. She is stopped by Freddie.

'Please, Ocean! Please! Bring my baby back!' she cries, fists clenched in terror.

Suddenly the tablet light is on again, seeming to glow brighter than ever. The screen bulges and then, with a strange slurping noise and a burst of light, Kylie is lying in a heap on the road as though she has just fallen upwards out of the screen. The crowd screams and gasps, and Melissa rushes forward.

'Kylie! Kylie! Are you all right? Where's Thomas? Is he with you?'

Kylie sits up, rubbing her head with both hands, then staggers to her feet. She blinks hard, then sees me. She moves her mouth but no words come out.

'Come on, Kylie. Come with me,' says Melissa, putting her arms round her, but Kylie shrugs her off.

'No, Aunty Mel. I'm staying right here till Thomas is back.' She turns to me. 'He will get back, won't he?'

I smile weakly. 'I hope so. Wh-where were you?'

'We were . . . here. Sort of.' She looks around and gestures disbelievingly at our surroundings. 'He was defending himself from a madman with an axe when I left. Oh sorry, Aunty Mel, it's just . . . Oh, I can't explain.'

I look at Kylie and say, 'How long have we got? Till . . . you know.'

'Till the Time Tablet doesn't work? I'd say five minutes. Bit longer maybe.'

'All right, listen up, everybody!' says Melissa, and I see the same look in her eyes as twenty-four hours ago – that time she marched through the gaggle of people in the studio and gathered me up. She is fierce, for sure.

'We need five minutes. That's all. Five minutes. This is my son we're talking about here so, if any of you –' she points her finger at the police – 'want to get your hands on *this* device, you're going to have to go through me first. Is that understood?'

She waits, then screams, '*Is that understood?*'

The Chief Constable frowns for a moment and then murmurs, 'Five minutes, Mrs Reeve.'

And so we wait, none of us in the slightest bit aware of what is happening in the twenty-fifth century.

CHAPTER 49

THOMAS

There are three of us left on the bridge – me, Pinker and Monsieur Lumière moaning in pain from his rebroken arm and badly wounded foot. We stand in a wide triangle, all of us transfixed by the sight of Pierre scaling the upright pillar of the bridge towards the high curved arch. Monsieur Lumière has pulled himself upright, the blood from his ankle wound forming a pool at his feet.

'Go after Pierre, Thomas. Only you can! And trust 'im!'

What can he mean? There's no way I can shin up there like a monkey. Pinker lurches forward with a growl and stretches out his meaty hand to grab my shoulder, but I dodge out of the way and start to run back the way we'd come. Pinker is old and overweight: he runs heavily and slowly. The two horsemen who'd been riding to the end of the bridge are there now, blocking my retreat. There, the arch of the bridge meets the road. There's only one way to escape them. I clamber up and on to the broad iron platform that slopes steeply upwards towards the top of the arch, fifty-five metres above the water.

Looking up, I can see that Pierre has already reached the top and is holding the Time Tablet towards me.

Can he know? Has he done this deliberately?

I can't look down. Instead, I fix my gaze on the metre-wide girders beneath me, with their flaking rust and corroded rivets and centuries of encrusted bird poo. I spread my arms to grip the sides and start to climb towards the top of the bridge. I climb quickly at first until I'm out of the reach of the horseman who has ridden towards me, grabbing at my ankle.

'You *idiot*!' Pinker bellows at him. ''Elp me up!'

I cast a look over my shoulder and see that Pinker has managed to haul himself on to the top span of the bridge as well and is following me, but much more slowly. If I just keep up my steady progress and don't look down . . .

I just looked down.

My stomach rose and fell like when you drive over a hump in the road, and I stare again at the bubbles of iron rust right in front of my face. I'm on my hands and knees, my arms wide, holding either side as I get higher and higher, the wind whipping my hair and clothes. I try not to think of how long it's been since the cathedral clock struck eight . . . Surely the Time Tablet will be losing its power soon?

'I'm gonna kill you!' bellows Pinker from about ten metres behind. I don't doubt for a second that he's telling the truth.

Ten metres? He's getting closer. I try to climb faster, but my legs are tired, and my hands are getting sore from gripping so tightly. Then I notice the climb getting a tiny bit less steep, which means I'm nearing the top of the curve.

I swallow hard and dare to look up. There, right ahead of me, is Pierre. And behind Pierre . . .

Is Duke. He too has climbed to the top of the bridge from the other side. He's not even holding on, but standing up. The slightest misstep would send him plunging to his death. When he sees me looking, he gives me a grin and shouts, 'Ships' masts, Tommo! That swine behind you used to send me up them till I had no fear of heights. Keep climbing!'

Between us, Pierre places the Time Tablet, still glowing, on the very apex of the bridge's curve, where it's level, and then shuffles back. 'Thanks, Pierre,' I say in my head because I'm not capable of actual speech right now.

It's there. Right in front of me. Two more metres and I can crawl into the screen. I hear a grunt behind me, and I feel a hand grab my foot.

I haven't come this far to give in now. I can't even see behind me, but I shake my foot free and scramble forward towards the Time Tablet. Duke steps carelessly over my prone body so that he's between me and Pinker.

Suddenly there's a ripping sound and a deafening creak, followed by a series of loud cracks. Beneath my chest, I feel the steel of the bridge trembling as dozens of 500-year-old iron rivets pop free, and a massive chunk of the bridge's arch begins to detach itself with Pinker still clinging on.

'No!' he wails. He stretches his arm over the widening gap, and his fingers connect with the section holding me and Duke.

''Elp me – oh please, 'elp me!'

But, even if Duke had wanted to, it's too late: that section of the bridge continues to creak and bend away. I see, to my horror, that Pierre is clinging desperately to the underside of the girder, unable to leap to safety.

I don't see the rest, for my attention is on the glowing light of the tablet, which seems to be fading. Stretching forward, I force my hand into the screen, and, as soon as I do, I find myself being sucked in.

'Good luck, Thomas! Send Ocean back!' is the second-to-last thing I hear in 2425. The last thing is Pierre's squeak of terror as the rotten girder that he and Pinker are clinging to falls towards the water below.

Then I get the rubber-band feeling again: stretched out almost to the point of breaking, and snapping back again, then landing me on the tarmac of the Tyne Bridge, surrounded by flashing blue lights.

There's a cheer, and the noise above my head of a helicopter, and then Mam's arms are round me. People have surged forward, and police officers are shouting, 'Stand back, stand back – give them all room!'

Then I see Ocean, and for a moment all the noise seems to retreat as she, Kylie and I stand there, gazing at one another. I find that I don't know what to say.

At our feet, the Time Tablet still glows, but less brightly. 'Did Pierre make it?' asks Kylie, and Ocean nods.

'That's good,' says Kylie. 'That's *ripper*. That means that Pinker *was* wrong. Your history hasn't ended. It's just that, from now on, we'll be on different paths. Good luck!'

There's no time for emotional goodbyes, even though this has been the most extraordinary journey ever. Instead, Ocean turns and hovers her foot over the Time Tablet. Then she steps into the the light and she's gone.

We're left staring at the Time Tablet on the ground as its light slowly fades.

Everyone seems to be in a sort of daze. Nobody's paying much heed when Kylie stoops and picks up the Time Tablet. Then, without warning, she draws back her arm and throws it over the side of the bridge. We watch it sail through the air and land in the purple river, too far below us to hear it splash. A gasp goes up around us, and mine is probably the loudest. Then I find myself gasping again as I'm lifted off the ground and wrapped in a massive embrace by Dad and Mam, who are both crying with relief.

'I've got to call your mum, Kylie,' says Mam, taking her phone out.

I point over the bridge at where Kylie had tossed the Time Tablet and say, 'What'd you do that for?'

'It's like I said, mate? We're now living a different future. That wretched device will never be buried under the yew tree. It won't now be dug up in four hundred and two years' time.'

'But . . . but that's not possible. How . . . I mean . . .?'

She looks at me slyly over the top of her specs. 'Not possible, Tommo? Where've you been for the last few days? Nothing's impossible in Everywhen. Let me explain . . .'

'Kylie, come and speak to your mum,' says Mam, and I'm kind of relieved. I don't think I could ever understand. Not properly.

CHAPTER 50

OCEAN

I open my eyes. I am lying on my back, staring at stars.

It is cold beneath my back and breezy. The events of the past few seconds are fresh in my mind. I know what has just happened, and I want to find out if I am back in 2425, but I know something is not right. Slowly, I roll over on to my side to push myself up, and I am nearly sick with terror as I see the water fifty metres below me. I lie back down and then, a moment later, I try again, even more slowly.

I am on top of the bridge. In my hand is Freddie's cellphone, which I tuck back into the pocket of my smock.

I hear Duke's voice and I lift my head to see him standing, careless, next to a massive gap in the bridge's span. 'Welcome back, Ocean. So bona ye made it! Now just grip the sides and you'll be kushti. There's no hurry. Pinker's . . . gone.' He points to the river below. 'And so has the Time Tablet.'

'G-gone? How?' I say.

'One second it was here, the next . . .' He shrugs. 'Mebbes Kylie did summink?'

Without looking down at the water, I manage to shuffle along on my bottom to a lower part of the arch, and crawl down that till I get closer and closer to where Monsieur Lumière is shouting, 'Ocean! Ocean! Slowly! Not too rapid-diddly!'

Then I am safely on the bridge with Duke and Monsieur Lumière, who looks absolutely ruined: pale, sick and bloody. He is shirtless: it looks as though he has used his shirt as a bandage to wrap round his foot; his arm is hanging limply by his side.

'Where is Nanny Moo?' I say.

'She . . . she stayed in the boat,' croaks Monsieur Lumière. The poor man is barely able to talk.

'And Pierre?' I ask.

Monsieur Lumière blinks hard and clears his throat. 'Pierre was a hero, you know?'

Was?

'He . . . he saved lives. Yours, Thomas's. Sadly, in order to do that . . .'

'Wait!' says Duke. 'Is that . . . is that Nanny Moo?'

Walking towards us in the twilight is Nanny Moo, and she is carrying something. When she gets closer, I can see she is soaking wet and that in her arms is a monkey – also wet, also exhausted, but nonetheless alive.

'*Oh là là! Il vive!* He is alive!' cries Monsieur Lumière, pulling himself upright and staggering towards them.

And then Nanny Moo has gathered me in her arms, and she is kissing my cheeks again and again.

'I saw Pinker and Pierre hit the water,' she says. 'Pinker broke Pierre's fall. I dived in all the same. I didn't see Pinker again, but I managed to save Pierre.'

The four of us all seem to be holding one another up.

'They've gone,' says Monsieur Lumière, looking behind us and across to the other side of the bridge. 'Pinker's men are not going to stick around.'

There is a small crowd of curious people on the other side, but they are drifting away as though embarrassed. I see Frau Schwartz among them.

Monsieur Lumière takes a long sip of ale, leans back and props up his freshly bandaged foot on the table in our front room. Nanny Moo tuts.

'If you're going to be staying here for good, Lumière, then there are a few rules. Like no feet on the furniture.'

For good? As in 'forever'? I look between Monsieur Lumière and Duke and Nanny Moo, and they all smile back at me as though they know something that I do not.

Monsieur Lumière takes his foot down and wipes the spot where it had been with a large silk handkerchief.

Then he waves it and it vanishes. (I think it goes up his sleeve, but I still do not know how it gets there.)

'Indubita-bubbly, madame. You are quite right.'

'You are staying?' I say.

'*Mais oui!* The travel-avelling life is over for me. At least for now. We will stay right here. And right *now*. After all, now that Frau Schwartz 'as left town, that library will need rebuilding.'

I look over at Duke. He is leaning against the doorframe, thumbs hooked in his waistcoat pockets. 'That means you are staying as well?'

He raps his feet rhythmically on the wooden floor, *rat-a-tat*, just like the first time we met. 'Sure I am. Might as well make a family, eh? And it's about time I went to school. Learn a bit more about that silicon chip you brought back in the cellphone. What do ye reckon?'

'I reckon,' I say, 'that that will be unbelieve-alieve-abubble!'

CHAPTER 51

THOMAS
THREE MONTHS LATER

We're about to drive over the Tyne Bridge when Kylie points to a road sign saying HEXHAM 24 MILES.

'Look – it's not that far to my school, Tommo,' she says. 'I'll come back at weekends. Can we stop on the bridge, Uncle Freddo?'

'Not really,' says Dad. 'I'll wait here. You two can walk. Don't be long or I'll get a ticket.'

And so we walk from the parked car to the centre of the massive bridge, four lanes of morning traffic roaring past us, and stop at exactly the point that our whole adventure in time ended.

'Oh jiminy. Head down, Tommo.'

Too late. A group of three teenagers – tourists, I guess – are coming from the opposite direction, and they stop when they see us and start talking animatedly in a language I don't understand.

One of them says, 'Hey! Hey! It's you! You! Ky-lee! Thomas! Ohmigod! Ohmigod!'

'Will this ever end, Kylie?' I groan.

'Smile and wave, Tommo. Smile and wave.'

'Can we get selfie? Can we get selfie?'

Not for the first time, nor the last, I pose with Kylie and the tourists, and say the same things.

'Yeah, it really happened,' I say.

'Yes – Andy and Des are really nice,' says Kylie.

'No, we've not been back to 2425.'

'No, I can't rebuild the Time Tablet.'

It's all they want, really. A few moments, a few selfies to prove that they've met *the* Kylie and Thomas. Once they've gone, we're alone again, staring down the Tyne at the Gateshead Millennium Bridge.

'Strange to think,' I say. 'Not a trace of that bridge will remain in four hundred years' time.'

Kylie laughs. 'You've still not understood, have you, Tommo? There's an infinite number of futures and . . .'

'Yeah, I get it. "Everywhen". That was just one possible future. It's still hard to get my head round, though. I'm not like you.'

We both turn at the sound of a honking horn. A white van is driving past with its window down. 'All right, kids! Kylie the Brain!' shouts the passenger. Kylie lifts her hand, a little wearily.

'Is that completely true, Kylie?' I say. 'That bit when

you say you can't rebuild the Time Tablet? That the old tablet that you got had a . . . a what? A "uniquely malfunctioning chip that cannot be replicated"?'

'Yeah. Good line that, eh?'

'Well?'

Kylie runs her hands through her tangle of curls and puffs out her cheeks. 'I've had enough of messing with time, Tommo? It was only meant to be a bit of fun. Besides, I've got plenty to be getting on with stopping that meteorite.'

'You sure you can do that?'

'Brain the size of a planet, mate! Thanks to that page you brought back, the North East Foundation Academy's already received a load of money from NASA, the ESA, the United Nations . . .'

'You never said.'

She shrugs. 'You never asked. Besides, it's kinda hush-hush. Too many people still think the whole thing was a stunt for TV, you know?'

I do know. Kylie and I have been invited back to Andy & Des's *Ministry of Mystery* show. Celia the producer has been very persuasive and offered us a large 'undisclosed sum' of money. Mam and Dad said no, and we didn't want to do it anyway.

Neither of us much likes being famous, it turns out.

'Was there a reason we got out of the car?' I say.

'Dunno. I just . . . felt drawn, you know? A feeling. Wanted to remind myself that it was real.'

I smile. 'Oh aye.' I tip my head back and get a surge in my stomach as I recall being on the very top of this bridge and hearing Pinker's scream as the rusty rivets gave way. It's a feeling that I fear will be with me for the rest of my life.

We're walking back to where Dad has parked on a double-yellow line, and there's a traffic warden with his little machine out ready to give him a ticket, when Dad points to us. The parking guy squints as we approach and then grins. 'Aa-aa-aa! Kylie an' Thom-aas!' He lowers his machine and wags his finger at Dad. 'This time I no give you ticket, hey? But maybe – nex' time – in the future! Ha ha ha!'

Dad says, 'Thanks, pal,' and, as we cross the bridge towards our own futures, I feel like we're leaving the past behind.

EPILOGUE

7 OCTOBER 2044

Thomas Reeve chose the day that the meteorite would have struck to get married. Of course, thanks to Professor Kylie T. Woollagong's revolutionary 'laser bees', that threat ended years ago. But Thomas's wife-to-be, Sarah, also thought it was quite cool.

The church at the end of the Long Sands was almost full. Thomas's mum, his dad, his Aunty Ailsa and many more relatives were in attendance, but Kylie had not turned up, even though she'd said she would. Thomas was disappointed, but told himself, *She is very busy.*

Kylie now lives in Sydney, Australia. As well as being the youngest-ever professor at the University of New South Wales, she's Director of the Wiki Universal Research Foundation.

'Will you, Thomas Frederick Reeve, take this woman . . .'

There was a loud bang from the back of the church as the wooden door crashed open. The whole congregation turned to see the commotion as a large woman in a bright yellow dress and matching Doc Marten boots, with twisty rust-coloured hair and big tinted glasses burst in and clomped to the end of the aisle.

'Ah, no worries, Tommo! Carry on, everyone! Sorry! Ruddy plane delayed, eh?'

Everyone laughed, and Kylie slipped into the rear pew next to a pair of grey-haired TV personalities who were sitting at the back so as not to attract attention.

Two minutes later, the vicar said, 'I now pronounce you man and wife.' A ripple of applause was punctuated by Kylie yelling, 'Oh ripper, mate! You did it!'

Thomas dragged his gaze from his new wife to look towards the back of the church.

'Well?' he said. 'Is she?'

Until now, Kylie had refused to tell Thomas whether his fiancée was the one she saw in the wedding photograph when they were both in 2425. She had texted him:

I'll tell you when you're married. You don't want to know.

Thomas was sure that he would have married Sarah anyway, but still – he *did* want to know, so he repeated the question while the guests looked on, curious.

Kylie drew out the moment, making Thomas sweat just for the fun of it.

'Oh yes, mate! She is very defin-efinitely the one in the photo!'

And even though they didn't understand exactly what

Kylie meant, when Thomas kissed his new wife – not easy when you're grinning – the whole congregation erupted in a frenzy of whoops and cheers, with Kylie cheering the loudest of all.

THE END

ACKNOWLEDGEMENTS

Any book is a collaborative work, and none of this would have been possible without the immense skill, patience and encouragement of a lot of people: far too many, in fact, to list here, but I'm going to name some anyway.

Principal among these are Nick Lake and Tom Bonnick at HarperCollins whose editorial guidance is so sharp yet painless: it's quite a feat to pull off and I am endlessly grateful for the trust they place in me.

Copyeditors have a unique skillset: they save authors from embarrassing mistakes like characters changing clothes mid-paragraph, or saying things out of character, or being in places (or centuries!) that would be impossible. Jane Tait is among the best and deserves special thanks.

Tom Clohosy Cole's name is always so undeservedly tiny on the back cover (look closely – it's there!). He's the brilliant cover artist, and with this wonderful cover he has excelled.

And finally, a HUGE thank you to the people who get my books into the hands of readers: the booksellers who recommend my books and the excellent teachers and librarians worldwide who play such an important part in any success my stories enjoy.

Thank you all!
RW

My dad died twice. But only the second
time was my fault.

Time Travelling
with a
Hamster

Ross Welford

Read on for a sneak peek of Ross Welford's
Time Travelling with a Hamster . . .

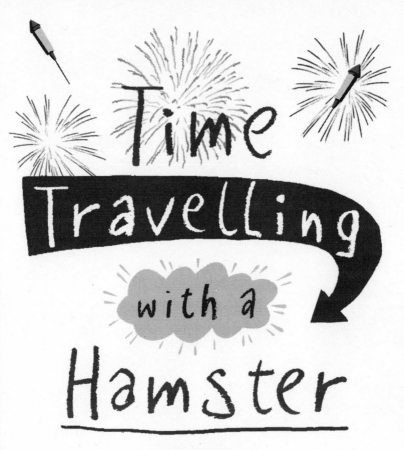

Time
Travelling
with a
Hamster

My dad died twice. Once when he was thirty-nine, and again four years later when he was twelve. (He's going to die a third time as well, which seems a bit rough on him, but I can't help that.)

The first time had nothing to do with me. The second time definitely did, but I would never even have been there if it hadn't been for his 'time machine'. I know – that sounds like I'm blaming him, which I'm totally not, but… you'll see what I mean.

I suppose if you'd asked me before, I'd have said a time machine might look something like a submarine? Or perhaps a space rocket. Anyway, something with loads of switches and panels and lights, made of iron or something, and big – I mean, *really* big, with thrusters, and boosters, and reactors…

Instead, I'm looking at a laptop and a tin tub from a garden centre.

This is my dad's time machine.

It's about to change the world – literally. Well, mine at any rate.

Chapter One

Just across the road from the house where we used to live before Dad died (the first time) is an alleyway that leads to the next street with a patch of grass with some bushes and straggly trees growing on it. I called it 'the jungle' when I was little, because in my mind that was what it was like, but looking at it now I can see that it's just a plot of land for a house that hasn't been built yet.

And that's where I am, still in my full-face motorbike helmet, sitting hidden in a bush in the dead of night, waiting to break into my old house.

There's an old fried-chicken box that someone's thrown there and I can smell something foul and sour, which I think might be fox's poo. The house is dark; there are no lights on. I'm looking up at my old bedroom window, the small one over the front door.

By day, Chesterton Road is pretty quiet – a long curve of small, semi-detached houses made of reddish bricks. When they were first built, they must all have looked exactly the same, but now people have added fancy gates, garage extensions, even a massive monkey-puzzle tree outside old Mr Frasier's, so these days they're all a bit different.

Now, at nearly one a.m., there's no one about and I've seen enough films and TV shows about criminals to know exactly how *not* to behave, and that's suspiciously. If you act normally, no one notices you. If I wandered nervously up and down the street waiting for the right time, then someone might spot me going backwards and forwards looking at the houses, and call the police.

On the other hand, if I'm just walking down the street, then that's all I'm doing, and it's as good as being invisible.

(Keeping the motorbike helmet on is a gamble, or what Grandpa Byron calls 'a calculated risk'. If I take it off, someone might notice that I'm nowhere near old enough to be riding a moped; if I keep it on, that looks suspicious – so I'm still in two minds about it. Anyway, it won't be on for long.)

I've worked all this out on the journey here. About a year ago, when we still lived here, the local council turned off every second streetlight in a money-saving experiment, so where I've stopped the moped it is really pretty dark.

As casually as I can, I come out of the bushes, take off the helmet and put it in the moped's top box. I pull my collar up and, without stopping, walk over the road to number 40. There I turn straight up the short driveway and stop in the shadows, well hidden by both the hedge that divides number 40's front garden from the one next door and the small Skoda that sits in the driveway.

So far, so good: the new owners of our house have not yet got round to fixing the garage doors. In fact, they're even less secure than they were. There's a brick in front of them to keep them shut, and when I crouch down and move it out of the way the right-hand door swings open, then bumps against the Skoda. For a dreadful moment I think the gap will be too small to let me in, but I just manage to squeeze through, and there I am, in the garage, which smells of dust and old oil. My torch is flashing round the walls to reveal boxes that they still haven't unpacked and, in the middle of the floor, the dark wooden planks covering up the cellar entrance.

Here's another tip if you're thinking of breaking in anywhere: don't flash your torch around too much. A flashing light will attract attention, whereas a still light doesn't. So I put my torch on the ground and start to lift up the greasy planks.

Under the planks there's a concrete stairway, and once I've gone down it I'm standing in a space about a metre square and to my right is a small metal door that's about half my height with a dusty, steel wheel for opening it like you get on ships. The wheel is secured into place by a stout bolt with a combination lock.

I try to give a little whistle of amazement, a "whew!", but my lips are so dry with nerves and dust that I can't.

Instead, I set the combination lock to the numbers Dad instructed in his letter – my birthday and month backwards – grab the wheel with both hands and twist it anti-clockwise. There's a bit of resistance but it gives with a soft grating noise, and as it spins around the door suddenly pops open inwards with a tiny sighing noise of escaping air.

I grab my torch and aim it ahead of me as I go through the little doorway, crouching. There are more steps down and a wall on my right and my hand finds a light switch but I daren't try it in case it's a switch for something else, like an alarm or something, or it lights up the garage upstairs, or… I just don't know, but I'm too nervous to flick the switch so I look at everything through the yellowy-white beam of torchlight.

The steps lead to a room about half the size of our living room at home, but with a lower ceiling. A grown-up could just about stand up.

Along one long wall are four bunk beds, all made up – blankets, pillows, everything. There's a wall that juts out into the room, and behind it is a toilet and some kind of machinery with pipes and hoses coming out of it. There are rugs on the white concrete floor and a poster on the wall. It's faded orange and black with a picture of a mum, a dad and two children inside a circle, and the words 'Protect And Survive' in big white letters. I've seen this poster before when some guy came to talk about peace and nuclear war and stuff in assembly once, and he'd made

Dania Biziewski cry because she was scared and he was really embarrassed.

This is what people built years ago when they thought Russia was going to kill us with nuclear bombs.

I turn round and see what's behind me. The torch beam picks out a long desk with a chair in front of it. On the desk is a tin tub, like you would bath a dog in or something. In it is an old-style Apple Mac laptop, the white one, and a computer mouse. There's a lead coming out of the back of the computer leading to a black metal box about the size of a paperback book, and coming out of that are two cords that are about a metre long, with strange sort of hand grips on the end.

Next to the tub is a coffee mug printed with a picture of me as a baby and the words 'I love my daddy'. The inside of the mug is all furred up with ancient mould.

And beside the mug is a copy of the local newspaper, the *Whitley Bay Advertiser*, folded in half and open at a story headlined 'Local Man's Tragic Sudden Death' above a picture of my dad.

I sit down in the swivel chair and run my hands over the underside of the desk. When I can't feel anything, I get on my knees and shine the torch upwards, and there it is: an envelope, taped at the back, just as Dad said there would be.

But there's no time machine. At least, not one that looks how I imagine a time machine might look.

That's how I end up staring at the tin tub and its contents.
Surely, I'm thinking, *Surely that's not it?*
But it is.
And the craziest thing? It works.